ALSO BY STUART DYBEK

*Childhood and Other Neighborhoods*

*Brass Knuckles*
(poetry)

## STUART DYBEK'S
# THE COAST OF CHICAGO

"The stories in *The Coast of Chicago* ... are fluently rendered scenes and dreams of a youth spent in the projects of Chicago.... Dybek's use of language [is] imaginative and precise ... a collection greater than the sum of its parts."
— *Philadelphia Inquirer*

"*The Coast of Chicago* is at times both tender and unforgiving. It is a balancing act between realism and the poetic, between youth and adulthood, between memory and an insistent present.... No matter where you grew up, after reading these stories you'll have found the coast of Chicago."
— *San Francisco Chronicle*

"Now and then a collection of stories achieves the virtues of both organic form and conciseness.... Dybek's book in fact stretches the definition of a short-story collection, reaching a kind of wholeness that gives it the feel of a novel."
— *Seattle Times*

"His vision is every inch his own."
— *USA Today*

# THE
# COAST
# OF
# CHICAGO

## STUART DYBEK

VINTAGE CONTEMPORARIES
VINTAGE BOOKS
A DIVISION OF RANDOM HOUSE, INC.
NEW YORK

FIRST VINTAGE CONTEMPORARIES EDITION, MARCH 1991

Some of these stories were originally published in somewhat
different form in *Alaska Quarterly Review, North American
Review, The Paris Review,* and *PEN Syndicated Fiction
Project. Antaeus:* "Hot Ice"; *Chicago:* "Chopin in Winter" and
"Blight"; *The New Yorker:* "Pet Milk"; *Ploughshares:* "Bijou";
*Triquarterly:* "Entry" (now titled "Farewell"), "Lights," "Strays,"
"Lost," and "Corks" (now titled "Bottle Caps").

Library of Congress Cataloging-in-Publication Data
Dybek, Stuart, 1942–
     The coast of Chicago / Stuart Dybek. — 1st Vintage
contemporaries ed.
          p.    cm. — (Vintage contemporaries)
     ISBN 0-679-73334-5 (pbk.)
     I. Title.
     [PS3554.Y3C6    1991]
     813'.54—dc20                                    90-50499
                                                          CIP

FOR MY BROTHERS, DAVE AND TOM

*Aż was, zjadacze chleba —*
*w aniołów przerobi.*

Until you lowly eaters of bread
Will be made into angels.

# Contents

# Acknowledgments

Some of these stories first appeared in somewhat different form in *The New Yorker, Antaeus, TriQuarterly, Ploughshares, Chicago Magazine, The North American Review, The Paris Review, PEN Syndicated Fiction Project, The Critic, Witness,* and *The Alaska Quarterly Review.* I wish to thank the editors of these magazines, and also the editors of the following anthologies, in which some of these stories have also appeared: *Prize Stories O. Henry Awards, New American Short Stories, The Pushcart Prize, X, The Ploughshares Reader: New Fiction for the Eighties, The Substance of Things Hoped For, Four Minute Fictions, The Graywolf Annual Four,* and *Sudden Fiction International.*

I also wish to express my gratitude to the Mrs. Giles Whiting Foundation, the Guggenheim Foundation, the National Endowment for the Arts, the Michigan Council for the Arts, and Western Michigan University for grants that provided the time during which these stories were

written. And I'd like personally to thank the Ponson
Estate for permission to use the painting reproduced on
the book jacket.

My thanks to Daniel Bourne for his translation of
the lines quoted in the dedication from *Testament mój*
by Juliusz Slowacki, and to Philip Levine for his translation of the epigraph by Antonio Machado.

*De toda la memoria, solo vale
el don preclare de evocar los suenos.*

— ANTONIO MACHADO

Out of the whole of memory, there's one thing
worthwhile: the great gift of calling back dreams.

# THE COAST OF CHICAGO

# FARWELL

Tonight, a steady drizzle, streetlights smoldering in fog like funnels of light collecting rain. Down Farwell, the balcony windows of the apartment building where my friend Babovitch once lived, reflected across the wet tennis courts, and I wondered if I would ever leave this city. I remembered the first night I walked down Farwell to visit Babo. He was teaching a class in Russian literature that I was taking, and had invited me over. I'd never had a teacher invite me to his home before. "When's a good time?" I asked.

"I can *always* use the company," he answered, scrawling out his address. "There's no phone."

It was a winter night, snowing. His apartment building was the last one on the block where the street dead-ended against the lake. Behind a snow-clotted cyclone fence, the tennis courts were drifted over, and beyond the courts and a small, lakeside park, a white pier extended to a green beacon. Snow had obliterated the outlines of sidewalks and curbs and that night the pier looked as if it was a continuation of the street, as if Farwell lengthened out into the lake. I walked out toward the beacon. Ice, sculpted by waves and spray, encrusted the pier. The guard cables and beacon tower were sheathed in ice. In the frozen quiet, I could hear the lake rasping in under the floes and feel the pier shudder, and as I walked back toward the apartment building I thought I heard singing.

The baritone voice resonating across the tennis courts seemed to float from a balcony window where a curtain fluttered out as if signalling. I was sure it was Babo's window. Instead of ringing his bell, I stood on the tennis court and tried to make out the song, but the words were indistinct. I formed a snowball out of fresh snow— snow too feathery to be good packing—and lobbed it at the window. It exploded against the pane with a soft *phoom*. I expected Babo to come to the window. Instead, the music stopped. I lobbed another snowball and the bronze light inside the apartment flicked off. Finally, I walked around to the entrance hall and buzzed the bell beside the name Andrei Babovitch, but there was no answer. I was about to give up when I saw his face magnified by the beveled panes of the lobby door. He opened the door and broke into the craggy grin I'd seen possess his face in class when he would read a poem aloud—first in Russian, as if chanting, and then translated into his hesitant, British-accented English.

"So, you," he said.

"Is it a good night for a visit?"

"Definitely. Come in, please. Have tea. And a little shot of something to warm up."

"I thought I guessed which window was yours and threw snowballs to get your attention."

"That was *you!* I thought hooligans had heard Chaliapin moaning about fate and become enraged. Russian opera can have that effect even on those not addicted to rock and roll. I didn't know what to expect next—a brick, maybe—so I turned off the music and laid down on the floor in the dark."

"Sorry," I said, "I wasn't thinking—I don't know why I didn't just ring the bell."

"No, no. It would have been a memorable entrance. I'm sorry I missed it, though if I looked out the window and saw you in the dark I still might have thought it was hooligans," he laughed. "As you see, my nerves aren't what they should be."

The bronze light was back on in his apartment, which seemed furnished in books. Books in various languages lined the walls and were stacked along the floor. His furniture was crates of more books, the stock left from a small Russian bookstore he'd opened then closed after receiving threats and a bomb in the mail. Above his desk, he'd tacked a street map of Odessa, where he'd grown up beside the Black Sea. There were circles of red ink along a few of the streets. I didn't ask that night, but later, when I knew him better, I asked what the red circles marked.

"Good bakeries," he said.

When the university didn't renew his contract, he moved away suddenly. It didn't surprise me. He'd been on the move since deserting to the British during the War. He'd lived in England, and Canada, and said he never knew where else was next, but that sooner or later staying in one place reminded him that where he belonged no longer existed. He'd lived on Farwell, a street whose name sounded almost like saying goodbye.

Tonight, I jogged down Farwell to the lake, past the puddled tennis courts and the pier with its green beacon, and then along the empty beach. Waves were rushing in and I ran as if being chased, tightroping along the foaming edge of water. My shoes peeled flying clods of footprints from the sand. It was late by the time I reached the building where I lived, the hallways quiet, supper smoke still ringing the lightbulbs. In the dark, my room with its windows raised smelled of wet screens and tangerines.

# CHOPIN IN WINTER

The winter Dzia-Dzia came to live with us in Mrs.
Kubiac's building on Eighteenth Street was the winter
that Mrs. Kubiac's daughter, Marcy, came home pregnant from college in New York. Marcy had gone there
on a music scholarship, the first person in Mrs. Kubiac's
family to go to high school, let alone college.

Since she had come home I had seen her only once. I
was playing on the landing before our door, and as she
came up the stairs we both nodded hi. She didn't look
pregnant. She was thin, dressed in a black coat, its
silvery fur collar pulled up around her face, her long
blonde hair tucked into the collar. I could see the snow-
flakes on the fur turning to beads of water under the hall
light bulb. Her face was pale and her eyes the same
startled blue as Mrs. Kubiac's.

She passed me almost without noticing and continued up the next flight of stairs, then paused and, leaning

over the banister, asked, "Are you the same little boy I used to hear crying at night?"

Her voice was gentle, yet kidding.

"I don't know," I said.

"If your name is Michael and if your bedroom window is on the fourth floor right below mine, then you are," she said. "When you were little sometimes I'd hear you crying your heart out at night. I guess I heard what your mother couldn't. The sound traveled up."

"I really woke you up?"

"Don't worry about that. I'm a very light sleeper. Snow falling wakes me up. I used to wish I could help you as long as we were both up together in the middle of the night with everyone else snoring."

"I don't remember crying," I said.

"Most people don't once they're happy again. It looks like you're happy enough now. Stay that way, kiddo." She smiled. It was a lovely smile. Her eyes seemed surprised by it. "Too-da-loo." She waved her fingers.

"Too-da-loo." I waved after her. A minute after she was gone I began to miss her.

Our landlady, Mrs. Kubiac, would come downstairs for tea in the afternoons and cry while telling my mother about Marcy. Marcy, Mrs. Kubiac said, wouldn't tell her who the child's father was. She wouldn't tell the priest. She wouldn't go to church. She wouldn't go anywhere. Even the doctor had to come to the house, and the only doctor that Marcy would allow was Dr. Shtulek, her childhood doctor.

"I tell her, 'Marcy, darling, you have to do something,'" Mrs. Kubiac said. "'What about all the sacrifices, the practice, the lessons, teachers, awards? Look at rich people—they don't let anything interfere with what they want.' "

Mrs. Kubiac told my mother these things in strictest confidence, her voice at first a secretive whisper, but growing louder as she recited her litany of troubles. The louder she talked the more broken her English became, as if her worry and suffering were straining the language past its limits. Finally, her feelings overpowered her; she began to weep and lapsed into Bohemian, which I couldn't understand.

I would sit out of sight beneath the dining-room table, my plastic cowboys galloping through a forest of chair legs, while I listened to Mrs. Kubiac talk about Marcy. I wanted to hear everything about her, and the more I heard the more precious the smile she had given me on the stairs became. It was like a secret bond between us. Once I became convinced of that, listening to Mrs. Kubiac seemed like spying. I was Marcy's friend and conspirator. She had spoken to me as if I was someone apart from the world she was shunning. Whatever her reasons for the way she was acting, whatever her secrets, I was on her side. In daydreams I proved my loyalty over and over.

At night we could hear her playing the piano—a muffled rumbling of scales that sounded vaguely familiar. Perhaps I actually remembered hearing Marcy practicing years earlier, before she had gone on to New York. The notes resonated through the kitchen ceiling while I wiped the supper dishes and Dzia-Dzia sat soaking his feet. Dzia-Dzia soaked his feet every night in a bucket of steaming water into which he dropped a tablet that fizzed, immediately turning the water bright pink. Between the steaming water and pink dye, his feet and legs, up to the knees where his trousers were rolled, looked permanently scalded.

Dzia-Dzia's feet seemed to be turning into hooves. His heels and soles were swollen nearly shapeless and cased in scaly calluses. Nails, yellow as a horse's teeth, grew gnarled from knobbed toes. Dzia-Dzia's feet had been frozen when as a young man he walked most of the way from Krakow to Gdansk in the dead of winter escaping service in the Prussian army. And later he had frozen them again mining for gold in Alaska. Most of what I knew of Dzia-Dzia's past had mainly to do with the history of his feet.

Sometimes my uncles would say something about him. It sounded as if he had spent his whole life on the move—selling dogs to the Igorot in the Philippines after the Spanish-American War; mining coal in Johnstown, Pennsylvania; working barges on the Great Lakes; riding the rails out West. No one in the family wanted much to do with him. He had deserted them so often, my uncle Roman said, that it was worse than growing up without a father.

My grandma had referred to him as *Pan Djabel*, "Mr. Devil," though the way she said it sounded as if he amused her. He called her a *gorel*, a hillbilly, and claimed that he came from a wealthy, educated family that had been stripped of their land by the Prussians.

"Landowners, all right!" Uncle Roman once said to my mother. "Besides acting like a bastard, according to Ma, he actually *was* one in the literal sense."

"Romey, shhh, what good's bitter?" my mother said.

"Who's bitter, Ev? It's just that he couldn't even show up to bury her. I'll never forgive that."

Dzia-Dzia hadn't been at Grandma's funeral. He had disappeared again, and no one had known where to find him. For years Dzia-Dzia would simply vanish without telling anyone, then suddenly show up out of nowhere to hang around for a while, ragged and smelling of liquor, wearing his two suits one over the other, only to disappear yet again.

"Want to find him? Go ask the bums on skid row," Uncle Roman would say.

My uncles said he lived in boxcars, basements, and abandoned buildings. And when, from the window of a bus, I'd see old men standing around trash fires behind billboards, I'd wonder if he was among them.

Now that he was very old and failing he sat in our kitchen, his feet aching and numb as if he had been out walking down Eighteenth Street barefoot in the snow.

It was my aunts and uncles who talked about Dzia-Dzia "failing." The word always made me nervous. I was failing, too—failing spelling, English, history, geography, almost everything except arithmetic, and that only because it used numbers instead of letters. Mainly, I was failing penmanship. The nuns complained that my writing was totally illegible, that I spelled like a DP, and threatened that if I didn't improve they might have to hold me back.

Mother kept my failures confidential. It was Dzia-Dzia's they discussed during Sunday visits in voices pitched just below the level of an old man's hearing. Dzia-Dzia stared fiercely but didn't deny what they were saying about him. He hadn't spoken since he had reappeared, and no one knew whether his muteness was caused by senility or stubbornness, or if he'd gone deaf. His ears had been frozen as well as his feet. Wiry white tufts of hair that matched his horned eyebrows sprouted from his ears. I wondered if he would hear better if they were trimmed.

Though Dzia-Dzia and I spent the evenings alone together in the kitchen, he didn't talk any more than he did on Sundays. Mother stayed in the parlor, immersed in her correspondence courses in bookkeeping. The piano rumbled above us through the ceiling. I could feel it more than hear it, especially the bass notes. Sometimes a chord would be struck that made the silverware clash in the drawer and the glasses hum.

Marcy had looked very thin climbing the stairs, delicate, incapable of such force. But her piano was massive and powerful-looking. I remembered going upstairs once with my mother to visit Mrs. Kubiac. Marcy was away at school then. The piano stood unused — top lowered, lid down over the keys — dominating the apartment. In the afternoon light it gleamed deeply, as if its dark wood were a kind of glass. Its pedals were polished bronze and looked to me more like pedals I imagined motormen stamping to operate streetcars.

"Isn't it beautiful, Michael?" my mother asked.

I nodded hard, hoping that Mrs. Kubiac would offer to let me play it, but she didn't.

"How did it get up here?" I asked. It seemed impossible that it could fit through a doorway.

"Wasn't easy," Mrs. Kubiac said, surprised. "Gave Mr. Kubiac a rupture. It come all the way on the boat from Europe. Some old German, a great musician, brang it over to give concerts, then got sick and left it. Went back to Germany. God knows what happened to him—I think he was a Jew. They auctioned it off to pay his hotel bill. That's life, huh? Otherwise who could afford it? We're not rich people."

"It must have been very expensive anyway," my mother said.

"Only cost me a marriage," Mrs. Kubiac said, then laughed, but it was forced. "That's life too, huh?" she asked. "Maybe a woman's better off without a husband?" And then, for just an instant, I saw her glance at my mother, then look away. It was a glance I had come to recognize from people when they caught themselves saying something that might remind my mother or me that my father had been killed in the war.

The silverware would clash and the glasses hum. I could feel it in my teeth and bones as the deep notes rumbled through the ceiling and walls like distant thunder. It wasn't like listening to music, yet more and more often I would notice Dzia-Dzia close his eyes, a look of concentration pinching his face as his body swayed slightly. I wondered what he was hearing. Mother had said once that he'd played the fiddle when she was a little girl, but the only music I'd even seen him show any interest in before was the "Frankie Yankovitch Polka Hour," which he turned up loud and listened to with his ear almost pressed to the radio. Whatever Marcy was playing, it didn't sound like Frankie Yankovitch.

Then one evening, after weeks of silence between us, punctuated only by grunts, Dzia-Dzia said, "That's boogie-woogie music."

"What, Dzia-Dzia?" I asked, startled.

"Music the boogies play."

"You mean from upstairs? That's Marcy."

"She's in love with a colored man."

"What are you telling him, Pa?" Mother demanded. She had just happened to enter the kitchen while Dzia-Dzia was speaking.

"About boogie-woogie." Dzia-Dzia's legs jiggled in the bucket so that the pink water sloshed over onto the linoleum.

"We don't need that kind of talk in the house."

"What talk, Evusha?"

"He doesn't have to hear that prejudice in the house," Mom said. "He'll pick up enough on the street."

"I just told him boogie-woogie."

"I think you better soak your feet in the parlor by the heater," Mom said. "We can spread newspaper."

Dzia-Dzia sat, squinting as if he didn't hear.

"You heard me, Pa. I said soak your feet in the parlor," Mom repeated on the verge of shouting.

"What, Evusha?"

"I'll yell as loud as I have to, Pa."

"Boogie-woogie, boogie-woogie, boogie-woogie," the old man muttered as he left the kitchen, slopping barefoot across the linoleum.

"Go soak your head while you're at it," Mom muttered behind him, too quietly for him to hear.

Mom had always insisted on polite language in the house. Someone who failed to say "please" or "thank you" was as offensive to her ears as someone who cursed.

"The word is 'yes,' not 'yeah,'" she would correct. Or "If you want 'hey,' go to a stable." She considered "ain't" a form of laziness, like not picking up your dirty socks.

Even when they got a little drunk at the family parties that took place at our flat on Sundays, my uncles tried not to swear—and they had all been in the army and the marines. Nor were they allowed to refer to the Germans as Krauts, or the Japanese as Nips. As far as Mom was concerned, of all the misuses of language, racial slurs were the most ignorant, and so the most foul.

My uncles didn't discuss the war much anyway, though whenever they got together there was a certain feeling in the room as if beneath the loud talk and joking they shared a deeper, sadder mood. Mom had replaced the photo of my father in his uniform with an earlier photo of him sitting on the running board of the car they'd owned before the war. He was grinning and petting the neighbor's Scottie. That one and their wedding picture were the only photos that Mom kept out. She knew I didn't remember my father, and she seldom talked about him. But there were a few times when she would read aloud parts of his letters. There was one passage in particular that she read at least once a year. It had been written while he was under bombardment, shortly before he was killed.

When it continues like this without letup you learn what it is to really hate. You begin to hate them as a people and want to punish them all— civilians, women, children, old people—it makes no difference, they're all the same, none of them innocent, and for a while your hate and anger keep you from going crazy with fear. But if you let yourself hate and believe in hate, then no matter what else happens, you've lost. Eve, I love our life together and want to come home to you and Michael, as much as I can, the same man who left.

I wanted to hear more but didn't ask. Perhaps because everyone seemed to be trying to forget. Perhaps because I was afraid. When the tears would start in Mom's eyes I caught myself wanting to glance away as Mrs. Kubiac had.

There was something more besides Mom's usual standards for the kind of language allowed in the house that caused her to lose her temper and kick Dzia-Dzia out of his spot in the kitchen. She had become even more sensitive, especially where Dzia-Dzia was concerned, because of what had happened with Shirley Popel's mother.

Shirley's mother had died recently. Mom and Shirley had been best friends since grade school, and after the funeral, Shirley came back to our house and poured out the story.

Her mother had broken a hip falling off a curb while sweeping the sidewalk in front of her house. She was a constantly smiling woman without any teeth who, everyone said, looked like a peasant. After forty years in America she could barely speak English, and even in the hospital refused to remove her babushka.

Everyone called her Babushka, Babush for short,

which meant "granny," even the nuns at the hospital. On top of her broken hip, Babush caught pneumonia, and one night Shirley got a call from the doctor saying Babush had taken a sudden turn for the worse. Shirley rushed right over, taking her thirteen-year-old son, Rudy. Rudy was Babushka's favorite, and Shirley hoped that seeing him would instill the will to live in her mother. It was Saturday night and Rudy was dressed to play at his first dance. He wanted to be a musician and was wearing clothes he had bought with money saved from his paper route. He'd bought them at Smoky Joe's on Maxwell Street—blue suede loafers, electric-blue socks, a lemon-yellow one-button roll-lapel suit with padded shoulders and pegged trousers, and a parrot-green satin shirt. Shirley thought he looked cute.

When they got to the hospital they found Babush connected to tubes and breathing oxygen.

"Ma," Shirley said, "Rudy's here."

Babush raised her head, took one look at Rudy, and smacked her gray tongue.

"Rudish," Babush said, "you dress like nigger." Then suddenly her eyes rolled; she fell back, gasped, and died.

"And those were her last words to any of us, Ev," Shirley wept, "words we'll carry the rest of our lives, but especially poor little Rudy—*you dress like nigger.*"

For weeks after Shirley's visit, no matter who called, Mom would tell them Shirley's story over the phone.

"Those aren't the kind of famous last words we're going to hear in this family if I can help it," she promised more than once, as if it were a real possibility. "Of course," she'd sometimes add, "Shirley always has let Rudy get away with too much. I don't see anything cute about a boy going to visit his grandmother at the hospital dressed like a hood."

Any last words Dzia-Dzia had he kept to himself. His silence, however, had already been broken. Perhaps in his own mind that was a defeat that carried him from failing to totally failed. He returned to the kitchen like a ghost haunting his old chair, one that appeared when I sat alone working on penmanship.

No one else seemed to notice a change, but it was clear from the way he no longer soaked his feet. He still kept up the pretense of sitting there with them in the bucket. The bucket went with him the way ghosts drag chains. But he no longer went through the ritual of boiling water: boiling it until the kettle screeched for mercy, pouring so the linoleum puddled and steam clouded around him, and finally dropping in the tablet that fizzed furiously pink, releasing a faintly metallic smell like a broken thermometer.

Without his bucket steaming, the fogged windows cleared. Mrs. Kubiac's building towered a story higher than any other on the block. From our fourth-story window I could look out at an even level with the roofs and see the snow gathering on them before it reached the street.

I sat at one end of the kitchen table copying down the words that would be on the spelling test the next day. Dzia-Dzia sat at the other, mumbling incessantly, as if finally free to talk about the jumble of the past he'd never mentioned—wars, revolutions, strikes, journeys to strange places, all run together, and music, especially Chopin. "Chopin," he'd whisper hoarsely, pointing to the ceiling with the reverence of nuns pointing to heaven. Then he'd close his eyes and his nostrils would widen as if he were inhaling the fragrance of sound.

It sounded no different to me, the same muffled thumping and rumbling we'd been hearing ever since Marcy had returned home. I could hear the intensity in the crescendos that made the silverware clash, but it never occurred to me to care what she was playing. What mattered was that I could hear her play each night, could feel her playing just a floor above, almost as if she were in our apartment. She seemed that close.

"Each night Chopin—it's all she thinks about, isn't it?"

I shrugged.

"You don't know?" Dzia-Dzia whispered, as if I were lying and he was humoring me.

"How should I know?"

"And I suppose how should you know the 'Grande Valse brillante' when you hear it either? How should you know Chopin was twenty-one when he composed it?—about the same age as the girl upstairs. He composed it in Vienna, before he went to Paris. Don't they teach you that in school? What are you studying?"

"Spelling."

"Can you spell *dummkopf*?"

The waves of the keyboard would pulse through the warm kitchen and I would become immersed in my spelling words, and after that in penmanship. I was in remedial penmanship. Nightly penmanship was like undergoing physical therapy. While I concentrated on the proper slant of my letters my left hand smeared graphite across the loose-leaf paper.

Dzia-Dzia, now that he was talking, no longer seemed content to sit and listen in silence. He would continually interrupt.

"Hey, Lefty, stop writing with your nose. Listen how she plays."

"Don't shake the table, Dzia-Dzia."

"You know this one? No? 'Valse brillante.' "

"I thought that was the other one."

"What other one? The E-flat? That's 'Grande Valse brillante.' This one's A-flat. Then there's another A-flat— Opus 42—called 'Grande Valse.' Understand?"

He rambled on like that about A- and E-flat and sharps and opuses and I went back to compressing my capital *M*'s. My homework was to write five hundred of them. I was failing penmanship yet again, my left hand, as usual, taking the blame it didn't deserve. The problem with *M* wasn't my hand. It was that I had never been convinced that the letters could all be the same widths. When I wrote, *M* automatically came out twice as broad as *N*, *H*, double the width of *I*.

"This was Paderewski's favorite waltz. She plays it like an angel."

I nodded, staring in despair at my homework. I had made the mistake of interconnecting the *M*'s into long strands. They hummed in my head, drowning out the music, and I wondered if I had been humming aloud. "Who's Paderewski?" I asked, thinking it might be one of Dzia-Dzia's old friends, maybe from Alaska.

"Do you know who's George Washington, who's Joe DiMaggio, who's Walt Disney?"

"Sure."

"I thought so. Paderewski was like them, except he

played Chopin. Understand? See, deep down inside, Lefty, you know more than you think."

Instead of going into the parlor to read comics or play with my cowboys while Mom pored over her correspondence courses, I began spending more time at the kitchen table, lingering over my homework as an excuse. My spelling began to improve, then took a turn toward perfection; the slant of my handwriting reversed toward the right; I began to hear melodies in what had sounded like muffled scales.

Each night Dzia-Dzia would tell me more about Chopin, describing the preludes or ballades or mazurkas, so that even if I hadn't heard them I could imagine them, especially Dzia-Dzia's favorites, the nocturnes, shimmering like black pools.

"She's playing her way through the waltzes," Dzia-Dzia told me, speaking as usual in his low, raspy voice as if we were having a confidential discussion. "She's young but already knows Chopin's secret—a waltz can tell more about the soul than a hymn."

By my bedtime the kitchen table would be shaking so much that it was impossible to practice penmanship any longer. Across from me, Dzia-Dzia, his hair, eyebrows, and ear tufts wild and white, swayed in his chair, with his eyes squeezed closed and a look of rapture on his face as his fingers pummeled the tabletop. He played the entire width of the table, his body leaning and twisting as his fingers swept the keyboard, left hand pounding at those chords that jangled silverware, while his right raced through runs across tacky oilcloth. His feet pumped the empty bucket. If I watched him, then closed my eyes, it sounded as if two pianos were playing.

One night Dzia-Dzia and Marcy played so that I expected at any moment the table would break and the ceiling collapse. The bulbs began to flicker in the overhead fixture, then went out. The entire flat went dark.

"Are the lights out in there, too?" Mom yelled from the parlor. "Don't worry, it must be a fuse."

The kitchen windows glowed with the light of snow. I looked out. All the buildings down Eighteenth Street were dark and the streetlights were out. Spraying wings of snow, a snow-removal machine, its yellow lights revolving, disappeared down Eighteenth like the last blinks of electricity. There wasn't any traffic. The block looked deserted, as if the entire city was deserted. Snow was filling the emptiness, big flakes floating steadily and softly between the darkened buildings, coating the fire escapes, while on the roofs a blizzard swirled up into the clouds.

Marcy and Dzia-Dzia never stopped playing.

"Michael, come in here by the heater, or if you're going to stay in there put the burners on," Mom called.

I lit the burners on the stove. They hovered in the dark like blue crowns of flame, flickering Dzia-Dzia's shadow across the walls. His head pitched, his arms flew up as he struck the notes. The walls and windowpanes shook with gusts of wind and music. I imagined plaster dust wafting down, coating the kitchen, a fine network of cracks spreading through the dishes.

"Michael?" Mother called.

"I'm sharpening my pencil." I stood by the sharpener grinding it as hard as I could, then sat back down and went on writing. The table rocked under my point, but the letters formed perfectly. I spelled new words, words I'd never heard before, yet as soon as I wrote them their meanings were clear, as if they were in another language, one in which words were understood by their sounds, like music. After the lights came back on I couldn't remember what they meant and threw them away.

Dzia-Dzia slumped back in his chair. He was flushed and mopped his forehead with a paper napkin.

"So, you liked that one," he said. "Which one was it?" he asked. He always asked me that, and little by little I had begun recognizing their melodies.

"The polonaise," I guessed. "In A-flat major."

"Ahhh," he shook his head in disappointment. "You think everything with a little spirit is the polonaise."

"The 'Revolutionary' étude!"

"It was a waltz," Dzia-Dzia said.

"How could that be a waltz?"

"A posthumous waltz. You know what 'posthumous' means?"

"What?"

"It means music from after a person's dead. The kind of waltz that has to carry back from the other side. Chopin wrote it to a young woman he loved. He kept his feelings for her secret but never forgot her. Sooner or later feelings come bursting out. The dead are as sentimental as anyone else. You know what happened when Chopin died?"

"No."

"They rang the bells all over Europe. It was winter. The Prussians heard them. They jumped on their horses. They had cavalry then, no tanks, just horses. They rode until they came to the house where Chopin lay on a bed next to a grand piano. His arms were crossed over his chest, and there was plaster drying on his hands and face. The Prussians rode right up the stairs and barged into the room, slashing with their sabers, their horses stamping and kicking up their front hooves. They hacked the piano and stabbed the music, then wadded up the music into the piano, spilled on kerosene from the lamps, and set it on fire. Then they rolled Chopin's piano to the window—it was those French windows, the kind that open out and there's a tiny balcony. The piano wouldn't fit, so they rammed it through, taking out part of the wall. It crashed three stories into the street, and when it hit it made a sound that shook the city. The piano lay there smoking, and the Prussians galloped over it and left. Later, some of Chopin's friends snuck back and removed his heart and sent it in a little jeweled box to be buried in Warsaw."

Dzia-Dzia stopped and listened. Marcy had begun to play again very faintly. If he had asked me to guess what she was playing I would have said a prelude, the one called "The Raindrop."

I heard the preludes on Saturday nights, sunk up to my ears in bathwater. The music traveled from upstairs through the plumbing, and resonated as clearly under-water as if I had been wearing earphones.

There were other places I discovered where Marcy's playing carried. Polonaises sometimes reverberated down an old trash chute that had been papered over in the dining room. Even in the parlor, provided no one else was listening to the radio or flipping pages of a news-paper, it was possible to hear the faintest hint of mazurkas around the sealed wall where the stovepipe from the space heater disappeared into what had once been a fireplace. And when I went out to play on the landing, bundled up as if I was going out to climb on the drifts piled along Eighteenth Street, I could hear the piano echoing down the hallways. I began to creep higher up the stairs to the top floor, until finally I was listening at Mrs. Kubiac's door, ready to jump away if it should suddenly open, hoping I would be able to think of some excuse for being there, and at the same time almost wishing they would catch me.

I didn't mention climbing the stairs in the hallway, nor any of the other places I'd discovered, to Dzia-Dzia. He never seemed interested in anyplace other than the kitchen table. It was as if he were attached to the chair, rooted in his bucket.

"Going so early? Where you rushing off to?" he'd ask at the end of each evening, no matter how late, when I'd put my pencil down and begun buckling my books into my satchel.

I'd leave him sitting there, with his feet in his empty bucket, and his fingers, tufted with the same white hair as his ears, still tracing arpeggios across the tabletop, though Marcy had already stopped playing. I didn't tell him how from my room, a few times lately after everyone was asleep, I could hear her playing as clearly as if I were sitting at her feet.

Marcy played less and less, especially in the evenings after supper, which had been her regular time.

Dzia-Dzia continued to shake the table nightly, eyes closed, hair flying, fingers thumping, but the thump of his fingers against the oilcloth was the only sound other than his breathing—rhythmic and labored as if he were having a dream or climbing a flight of stairs.

I didn't notice at first, but Dzia-Dzia's solos were the start of his return to silence.

"What's she playing, Lefty?" he demanded more insistently than ever, as if still testing whether I knew.

Usually now, I did. But after a while I realized he was no longer testing me. He was asking because the sounds were becoming increasingly muddled to him. He seemed able to feel the pulse of the music but could no longer distinguish the melodies. By asking me, he hoped perhaps that if he knew what Marcy was playing he would hear it clearly himself.

Then he began to ask what she was playing when she wasn't playing at all.

I would make up answers. "The polonaise . . . in A-flat major."

"The polonaise! You always say that. Listen harder. Are you sure it's not a waltz?"

"You're right, Dzia-Dzia. It's the 'Grande Valse'."

"The 'Grande Valse' . . . which one is that?"

"A-flat, Opus 42. Paderewski's favorite, remember? Chopin wrote it when he was twenty-one, in Vienna."

"In Vienna?" Dzia-Dzia asked, then pounded the table with his fist. "Don't tell me numbers and letters! A-flat, Z-sharp, Opus 0, Opus 1,000! Who cares? You make it sound like a bingo game instead of Chopin."

I was never sure if he couldn't hear because he couldn't remember, or couldn't remember because he couldn't hear. His hearing itself still seemed sharp enough.

"Stop scratching with that pencil all the time, Lefty, and I wouldn't have to ask you what she's playing," he'd complain.

"You'd hear better, Dzia-Dzia, if you'd take the kettle off the stove."

He was slipping back into his ritual of boiling water. The kettle screeched like a siren. The windows fogged. Roofs and weather vanished behind a slick of steam. Vapor ringed the overhead light bulbs. The vaguely metallic smell of the fizzing pink tablets hung at the end of every breath.

Marcy played hardly at all by then. What little she played was muffled, far off as if filtering through the same fog. Sometimes, staring at the steamed windows, I imagined Eighteenth Street looked that way, with rings of vapor around the streetlights and headlights, clouds billowing from exhaust pipes and manhole covers, breaths hanging, snow swirling like white smoke.

Each night water hissed from the kettle's spout as from a blown valve, rumbling as it filled the bucket, brimming until it slopped over onto the warped linoleum. Dzia-Dzia sat, bony calves half submerged, trousers rolled to his knees. He was wearing two suits again, one over the other, always a sure sign he was getting ready to travel, to disappear without saying good-bye. The fingers of his left hand still drummed unconsciously along the tabletop as his feet soaked. Steam curled up the arteries of his scalded legs, hovered over his lap, smoldered up the buttons of his two vests, traced his mustache and white tufts of hair until it enveloped him. He sat in a cloud, eyes glazed, fading.

.   .   .

I began to go to bed early. I would leave my homework unfinished, kiss Mother good night, and go to my room.

My room was small, hardly space for more than the bed and bureau. Not so small, though, that Dzia-Dzia couldn't have fit. Perhaps, had I told him that Marcy played almost every night now after everyone was sleeping, he wouldn't have gone back to filling the kitchen with steam. I felt guilty, but it was too late, and I shut the door quickly before steam could enter and fog my window.

It was a single window. I could touch it from the foot of the bed. It opened onto a recessed, three-sided air shaft and faced the roof of the building next door. Years ago a kid my age named Freddy had lived next door and we still called it Freddy's roof.

Marcy's window was above mine. The music traveled down as clearly as Marcy said my crying had traveled up. When I closed my eyes I could imagine sitting on the Oriental carpet beside her huge piano. The air shaft actually amplified the music just as it had once amplified the arguments between Mr. and Mrs. Kubiac, especially the shouting on those nights after Mr. Kubiac had moved out, when he would return drunk and try to move back in. They'd argued mostly in Bohemian, but when Mr. Kubiac started beating her, Mrs. Kubiac would yell out in English, "Help me, police, somebody, he's killing me!" After a while the police would usually come and haul Mr. Kubiac away. I think sometimes Mom called them. One night Mr. Kubiac tried to fight off the police, and they gave him a terrible beating. "You're killing him in front of my eyes!" Mrs. Kubiac began to scream. Mr. Kubiac broke away and, with the police chasing him, ran down the hallways pounding on doors, pleading for people to open up. He pounded on our door. Nobody in the building let him in. That was their last argument.

The room was always cold. I'd slip, still wearing my clothes, under the goose-feather–stuffed *piersyna* to change into my pajamas. It would have been warmer with the door open even a crack, but I kept it closed because of the steam. A steamed bedroom window reminded me too much of the winter I'd had pneumonia. It was one of the earliest things I could remember: the gurgling hiss of the vaporizer and smell of benzoin while I lay sunk in my pillows watching steam condense to frost on the pane until daylight blurred. I could remember trying to scratch through the frost with the key to a windup mouse so that I could see how much snow had fallen, and Mother catching me. She was furious that I had climbed out from under the warmth of my covers and asked me if I wanted to get well or to get sicker and die. Later, when I asked Dr. Shtulek if I was dying, he put his stethoscope to my nose and listened. "Not yet." He smiled. Dr. Shtulek visited often to check my breathing. His stethoscope was cold like all the instruments in his bag, but I liked him, especially for unplugging the vaporizer. "We don't need this anymore," he confided. Night seemed very still without its steady exhaling. The jingle of snow chains and the scraping of shovels carried from Eighteenth Street. Maybe that was when I first heard Marcy practicing scales. By then I had grown used to napping during the day and lying awake at night. I began to tunnel under my *piersyna* to the window and scrape at the layered frost. I scraped for nights, always

afraid I would get sick again for disobeying. Finally, I
was able to see the snow on Freddy's roof. Something
had changed while I'd been sick—they had put a wind
hood on the tall chimney that sometimes blew smoke
into our flat. In the dark it looked as if someone was
standing on the roof in an old-fashioned helmet. I imagined it was a German soldier. I'd heard Freddy's land-
lord was German. The soldier stood at attention, but his
head slowly turned back and forth and hooted with
each gust of wind. Snow drove sideways across the roof,
and he stood banked by drifts, smoking a cigar. Sparks
flew from its tip. When he turned completely around to
stare in my direction with his faceless face, I'd duck and
tunnel back under my *piersyna* to my pillows and pretend to sleep. I believed a person asleep would be shown
more mercy than a person awake. I'd lie still, afraid he
was marching across the roof to peer in at me through
the holes I'd scraped. It was a night like that when I
heard Mother crying. She was walking from room to
room crying like I'd never heard anyone cry before.
I must have called out because she came into my room
and tucked the covers around me. "Everything will be
all right," she whispered; "go back to sleep." She sat on
my bed, toward the foot where she could look out the
window, crying softly until her shoulders began to shake.
I lay pretending to sleep. She cried like that for nights
after my father was killed. It was my mother, not I,
whom Marcy had heard.

It was only after Marcy began playing late at night that I
remembered my mother crying. In my room, with the
door shut against the steam, it seemed she was playing

for me alone. I would wake already listening and gradually realize that the music had been going on while I slept, and that I had been shaping my dreams to it. She played only nocturnes those last weeks of winter. Sometimes they seemed to carry over the roofs, but mostly she played so softly that only the air shaft made it possible to hear. I would sit huddled in my covers beside the window listening, looking out at the white dunes on Freddy's roof. The soldier was long gone, his helmet rusted off. Smoke blew unhooded; black flakes with sparking edges wafted out like burning snow. Soot and music and white gusts off the crests buffeted the pane. Even when the icicles began to leak and the streets to turn to brown rivers of slush, the blizzard in the air shaft continued.

Marcy disappeared during the first break in the weather. She left a note that read: "Ma, don't worry."

"That's all," Mrs. Kubiac said, unfolding it for my mother to see. "Not even 'love,' not even her name signed. The whole time I kept telling her 'do something,' she sits playing the piano, and now she does something, when it's too late, unless she goes to some butcher. Ev, what should I do?"

My mother helped Mrs. Kubiac call the hospitals. Each day they called the morgue. After a week, Mrs. Kubiac called the police, and when they couldn't find Marcy, any more than they had been able to find Dzia-Dzia, Mrs. Kubiac began to call people in New York— teachers, old roommates, landlords. She used our phone. "Take it off the rent," she said. Finally, Mrs. Kubiac went to New York herself to search.

When she came back from New York she seemed

changed, as if she'd grown too tired to be frantic. Her hair was a different shade of gray so that now you'd never know it had once been blonde. There was a stoop to her shoulders as she descended the stairs on the way to novenas. She no longer came downstairs for tea and long talks. She spent much of her time in church, indistinguishable among the other women from the old country, regulars at the morning requiem mass, wearing babushkas and dressed in black like a sodality of widows, droning endless mournful litanies before the side altar of the Black Virgin of Czestochowa.

By the time a letter from Marcy finally came, explaining that the entire time she had been living on the South Side in a Negro neighborhood near the university, and that she had a son whom she'd named Tatum Kubiac—"Tatum" after a famous jazz pianist—it seemed to make little difference. Mrs. Kubiac visited once but didn't go back. People had already learned to glance away from her when certain subjects were mentioned—daughters, grandchildren, music. She had learned to glance away from herself. After she visited Marcy she tried to sell the piano, but the movers couldn't figure how to get it downstairs, nor how anyone had ever managed to move it in.

It took time for the music to fade. I kept catching wisps of it in the air shaft, behind walls and ceilings, under bathwater. Echoes traveled the pipes and wallpapered chutes, the bricked-up flues and dark hallways. Mrs. Kubiac's building seemed riddled with its secret passageways. And, when the music finally disappeared, its channels remained, conveying silence. Not an ordinary silence of absence and emptiness, but a pure silence beyond daydream and memory, as intense as the music it replaced, which, like music, had the power to change whoever listened. It hushed the close-quartered racket of the old building. It had always been there behind the creaks and drafts and slamming doors, behind the staticky radios, and the flushings and footsteps and crackling fat, behind the wails of vacuums and kettles and babies, and the voices with their scraps of conversation and arguments and laughter floating out of flats where people locked themselves in with all that was private. Even after I no longer missed her, I could still hear the silence left behind.

# LIGHTS

In summer, waiting for night, we'd pose against the afterglow on corners, watching traffic cruise through the neighborhood. Sometimes, a car would go by without its headlights on and we'd all yell, "Lights!"

"Lights!" we'd keep yelling until the beams flashed on. It was usually immediate—the driver honking back thanks, or flinching embarrassed behind the steering wheel, or gunning past, and we'd see his red taillights blink on.

But there were times—who knows why?—when drunk or high, stubborn, or simply lost in that glide to somewhere else, the driver just kept driving in the dark, and all down the block we'd hear yelling from doorways and storefronts, front steps, and other corners, voices winking on like fireflies: "Lights! Your *lights*! Hey, lights!"

# DEATH OF
# THE RIGHT FIELDER

After too many balls went out and never came back we went out to check. It was a long walk—he always played deep. Finally we saw him, from the distance resembling the towel we sometimes threw down for second base.

It was hard to tell how long he'd been lying there, sprawled on his face. Had he been playing infield, his presence, or lack of it, would, of course, have been noticed immediately. The infield demands communication—the constant, reassuring chatter of team play. But he was remote, clearly an outfielder (the temptation is to say out-*sider*). The infield is for wisecrackers, pepper-pots, gum-poppers; the outfield is for loners, onlookers, brooders who would rather study clover and swat gnats than holler. People could pretty much be divided between infielders and outfielders. Not that one always has a choice. He didn't necessarily choose right field so much as accept it.

There were several theories as to what killed him.

From the start the most popular was that he'd been shot. Perhaps from a passing car, possibly by that gang calling themselves the Jokers, who played sixteen-inch softball on the concrete diamond with painted bases in the center of the housing project, or by the Latin Lords, who didn't play sports, period. Or maybe some pervert with a telescopic sight from a bedroom window, or a mad sniper from a water tower, or a terrorist with a silencer from the expressway overpass, or maybe it was an accident, a stray slug from a robbery, or shoot-out, or assassination attempt miles away.

No matter who pulled the trigger it seemed more plausible to ascribe his death to a bullet than to natural causes like, say, a heart attack. Young deaths are never natural; they're all violent. Not that kids don't die of heart attacks. But he never seemed the type. Sure, he was quiet, but not the quiet of someone always listening for the heart murmur his family repeatedly warned him about since he was old enough to play. Nor could it have been leukemia. He wasn't a talented enough athlete to die of that. He'd have been playing center, not right, if leukemia was going to get him.

The shooting theory was better, even though there wasn't a mark on him. Couldn't it have been, as some argued, a high-powered bullet traveling with such velocity that its hole fuses behind it? Still, not everyone was satisfied. Other theories were formulated, rumors became legends over the years: he'd had an allergic reaction to a bee sting, been struck by a single bolt of lightning from a freak, instantaneous electrical storm, ingested too strong a dose of insecticide from the grass blades he chewed on, sonic waves, radiation, pollution, etc. And a few of us liked to think it was simply that chasing a sinking liner, diving to make a shoestring catch, he broke his neck.

There *was* a ball in the webbing of his mitt when we turned him over. His mitt had been pinned under his body and was coated with an almost luminescent gray film. There was the same gray on his black, high-top gym shoes, as if he'd been running through lime, and along the bill of his baseball cap — the blue felt one with the red *C* which he always denied stood for the Chicago Cubs. He may have been a loner, but he didn't want to be identified with a loser. He lacked the sense of humor for that, lacked the perverse pride that sticking for losers season after season breeds, and the love. He was just an ordinary guy, .250 at the plate, and we stood above him not knowing what to do next. By then the guys from the other outfield positions had trotted over. Someone, the shortstop probably, suggested team prayer. But no one could think of a team prayer. So we all just stood there silently bowing our heads, pretending to pray while the shadows moved darkly across the outfield grass. After a while the entire diamond was swallowed and the field lights came on.

In the bluish squint of those lights he didn't look like someone we'd once known — nothing looked quite right — and we hurriedly scratched a shallow grave, covered him over, and stamped it down as much as possible so that the next right fielder, whoever he'd be, wouldn't trip. It could be just such a juvenile, seemingly trivial stumble that would ruin a great career before it had begun, or hamper it years later the way Mantle's was hampered by bum knees. One can never be sure the kid beside him isn't another Roberto Clemente; and who can ever know how many potential Great Ones have gone down in the obscurity of their neighborhoods? And so, in the catcher's phrase, we "buried the grave" rather than contribute to any further tragedy. In all likelihood the next right fielder, whoever he'd be, would be clumsy too, and if there was a mound to trip over he'd find it and break *his* neck, and soon right field would get the reputation as haunted, a kind of sandlot Bermuda Triangle, inhabited by phantoms calling for ghostly fly balls, where no one but the most desperate outcasts, already on the verge of suicide, would be willing to play.

Still, despite our efforts, we couldn't totally disguise it. A fresh grave is stubborn. Its outline remained visible—a scuffed bald spot that might have been confused for an aberrant pitcher's mound except for the bat jammed in the earth with the mitt and blue cap fit over it. Perhaps we didn't want to eradicate it completely—a part of us was resting there. Perhaps we wanted the new right fielder, whoever he'd be, to notice and wonder about who played there before him, realizing he was now the only link between past and future that mattered. A monument, epitaph, flowers, wouldn't be necessary.

As for us, we walked back, but by then it was too late—getting on to supper, getting on to the end of summer vacation, time for other things, college, careers, settling down and raising a family. Past thirty-five the talk starts about being over the hill, about a graying Phil Niekro in his forties still fanning them with the knuckler as if it's some kind of miracle, about Pete Rose still going in headfirst at forty, beating the odds. And maybe the talk is right. One remembers Willie Mays, forty-two years old and a Met, dropping that can-of-corn fly in the

'73 Series, all that grace stripped away and with it the conviction, leaving a man confused and apologetic about the boy in him. It's sad to admit it ends so soon, but everyone knows those are the lucky ones. Most guys are washed up by seventeen.

# BOTTLE CAPS

Each day I'd collect caps from beer bottles. I'd go early in the morning through the alleys with a shopping bag, the way I'd seen old women and bums, picking through trash in a cloud of flies. Collectors of all kinds thrived in the alleys: scrap collectors, deposit-bottle collectors, other-people's-hubcap collectors. I made my rounds, stopping behind taverns where bottle caps spilled from splitting, soggy bags—clinking, shiny heaps, still sudded with beer, clotted with cigarette ashes from the night before.

I'd hose them down and store them in coffee cans. At the end of the week, I'd line up my bottle caps for contests between the brands. It was basically a three-way race between Pabst, with its blue-ribboned cap, Bud, and Miller. Blatz and Schlitz weren't far behind.

That got boring fast. It was the rare and exotic bottle caps that kept me collecting—Edelweiss; Yusay Pilsner; Carling's Black Label, with its matching black cap; Monarch, from the brewery down the street, its gold caps like pieces of eight; and Meister Brau Bock, my favorite, each cap a ram's-head medallion.

By July, I had too many to count. The coffee cans stashed in the basement began to smell—a metallic, fermenting malt. I worried my mother would find out. It would look to her as if I were brewing polio. Still, the longer I collected, the more I hoarded my bottle caps. They had come to seem almost beautiful. It fascinated me how some were lined with plastic, some with foil. I noticed how only the foreign caps were lined with cork. I tapped the dents from those badly mangled by openers. When friends asked for bottle caps to decorate the spokes on their bikes, I refused.

One afternoon I caught my younger brother in the basement, stuffing my bottle caps into his pocket.

"What do you think you're doing?" I demanded.

At first he wouldn't talk, but I had him by the T-shirt, which I worked up around his throat, slowly twisting it to a knot at his windpipe.

He led me into the backyard, to a sunless patch behind the oil shed, and pointed. Everywhere I looked I could see my bottle caps half buried, their jagged edges sticking up among clothespin crosses and pieces of colored glass.

"I've been using them as tombstones," he said, "in my insect graveyard."

# BLIGHT

During those years between Korea and Vietnam, when rock and roll was being perfected, our neighborhood was proclaimed an Official Blight Area.

Richard J. Daley was mayor then. It seemed as if he had always been, and would always be, the mayor. Ziggy Zilinsky claimed to have seen the mayor himself riding down Twenty-third Place in a black limousine flying one of those little purple pennants from funerals, except his said WHITE SOX on it. The mayor sat in the backseat sorrowfully shaking his head as if to say "Jeez!" as he stared out the bulletproof window at the winos drinking on the corner by the boarded-up grocery.

Of course, nobody believed that Zig had actually seen the mayor. Ziggy had been unreliable even before Pepper Rosado had accidentally beaned him during a game of "it" with the bat. People still remembered as far back as third grade when Ziggy had jumped up in the middle of mass yelling, "Didja see her? She nodded! I asked the Blessed Virgin would my cat come home and she nodded yes!"

All through grade school the statues of saints winked at Ziggy. He was in constant communication with angels and the dead. And Ziggy sleepwalked. The cops had picked him up once in the middle of the night for running around the bases in Washtenaw Playground while still asleep.

When he'd wake up, Ziggy would recount his dreams as if they were prophecies. He had a terrible recurring nightmare in which atomic bombs dropped on the city the night the White Sox won the pennant. He could see the mushroom cloud rising out of Comiskey Park. But Zig had wonderful dreams, too. My favorite was the one in which he and I and Little Richard were in a band playing in the center of St. Sabina's roller rink.

After Pepper brained him out on the boulevard with a bat—a fungo bat that Pepper whipped like a tomahawk across a twenty-yard width of tulip garden that Ziggy was trying to hide behind—Zig stopped seeing visions of the saints. Instead, he began catching glimpses of famous people, not movie stars so much as big shots in the news. Every once in a while Zig would spot somebody like Bo Diddley going by on a bus. Mainly, though, it would be some guy in a homburg who looked an awful lot like Eisenhower, or he'd notice a reappearing little gray-haired fat guy who could turn out to be either Nikita Khrushchev or Mayor Daley. It didn't surprise us. Zig was the kind of kid who read newspapers. We'd all go to Potok's to buy comics and Zig would walk out with the *Daily News*. Zig had always worried about things no one else cared about, like the population explosion, people starving in India, the world blowing up. We'd be walking along down Twenty-second and pass an alley and Ziggy would say, "See that?"

"See what?"

"Mayor Daley scrounging through garbage."

We'd all turn back and look but only see a bag lady picking through cans.

Still, in a way, I could see it from Ziggy's point of view. Mayor Daley *was* everywhere. The city was tearing down buildings for urban renewal and tearing up streets for a new expressway, and everywhere one looked there were signs in front of the rubble reading:

SORRY FOR THE INCONVENIENCE
ANOTHER IMPROVEMENT
FOR A GREATER CHICAGO
RICHARD J. DALEY, MAYOR

Not only were there signs everywhere, but a few blocks away a steady stream of fat, older, bossy-looking guys emanated from the courthouse on Twenty-sixth. They looked like a corps of Mayor Daley doubles, and sometimes, especially on election days, they'd march into the neighborhood chewing cigars and position themselves in front of the flag-draped barbershops that served as polling places.

But back to blight.

That was an expression we used a lot. We'd say it after going downtown, or after spending the day at the Oak Street Beach, which we regarded as the beach of choice for sophisticates. We'd pack our towels and, wearing our swimsuits under our jeans, take the subway north.

"North to freedom," one of us would always say.

Those were days of longing without cares, of nothing to do but lie out on the sand inspecting the world from behind our sunglasses. At the Oak Street Beach the city seemed to realize our dreams of it. We gazed out nonchalantly at the white-sailed yachts on the watercolor-blue horizon, or back across the Outer Drive at the lake-reflecting glass walls of high rises as if we took such splendor for granted. The blue, absorbing shadow would deepen to azure, and a fiery orange sun would dip behind the glittering buildings. The crowded beach would gradually empty, and a pitted moon would hover over sand scalloped with a million footprints. It would be time to go.

"Back to blight," one of us would always joke.

I remember a day shortly after blight first became official. We were walking down Rockwell, cutting through the truck docks, Zig, Pepper, and I, on our way to the viaduct near Douglas Park. Pepper was doing his Fats Domino impression, complete with opening piano riff: *Bum-pah-da bum-pa-da dummmmm* . . .

> *Ah foun' mah thrill*
> *Ahn Blueberry Hill* . . .

It was the route we usually walked to the viaduct, but since blight had been declared we were trying to see our surroundings from a new perspective, to determine if anything had been changed, or at least appeared different. Blight sounded serious, biblical in a way, like something locusts might be responsible for.

"Or a plague of gigantic, radioactive cockroaches," Zig said, "climbing out of the sewers."

"Blight, my kabotch," Pepper said, grabbing his kabotch and shaking it at the world. "They call this blight? Hey, man, there's weeds and trees and everything, man. You shoulda seen it on Eighteenth Street."

We passed a Buick somebody had dumped near the railroad tracks. It had been sitting there for months and was still crusted with salt-streaked winter grime. Someone had scraped WASH ME across its dirty trunk, and someone else had scrawled WHIP ME across its hood. Pepper snapped off the aerial and whipped it back and forth so that the air whined, then slammed it down on a fender and began rapping out a Latin beat. We watched him smacking the hell out of it, then Zig and I picked up sticks and broken hunks of bricks and started clanking the headlights and bumpers as if they were bongos and congas, all of us chanting out the melody to "Tequila." Each time we grunted out the word *tequila*, Pepper, who was dancing on the hood, stomped out more windshield.

We were revving up for the viaduct, a natural echo chamber where we'd been going for blues-shout contests ever since we'd become infatuated with Screamin' Jay Hawkins's "I Put a Spell on You." In fact, it was practicing blues shouts together that led to the formation of our band, the No Names. We practiced in the basement of the apartment building I lived in: Zig on bass, me on sax, Pepper on drums, and a guy named Deejo who played accordion, though he promised us he was saving up to buy an electric guitar.

Pepper could play. He was a natural.

"I go crazy," was how he described it.

His real name was Stanley Rosado. His mother sometimes called him Stashu, which he hated. She was Polish and his father was Mexican—the two main nationalities in the neighborhood together in one house. It wasn't always an easy alliance, especially inside Pepper. When he got pissed he was a wild man. Things suffered, sometimes people, but always things. Smashing stuff seemed to fill him with peace. Sometimes he didn't even realize he was doing it, like the time he took flowers to Linda Molina, a girl he'd been nuts about since grade school. Linda lived in one of the well-kept two-flats along Marshall Boulevard, right across from the Assumption Church. Maybe it was just that proximity to the church, but there had always been a special aura about her. Pepper referred to her as "the Unadulterated One." He finally worked up the nerve to call her, and when she actually invited him over, he walked down the boulevard to her house in a trance. It was late spring, almost summer, and the green boulevard stretched like an enormous lawn before Linda Molina's house. At its center was a blazing garden of tulips. The city had planted them. Their stalks sprouted tall, more like corn than flowers, and their colors seemed to vibrate in the air. The tulips were the most beautiful thing in the neighborhood. Mothers wheeled babies by them; old folks hobbled for blocks and stood before the flowers as if they were sacred.

Linda answered the door and Pepper stood there holding a huge bouquet. Clumps of dirt still dangled from the roots.

"For you," Pepper said.

Linda, smiling with astonishment, accepted the

flowers; then her eyes suddenly widened in horror. "You didn't—?" she asked.

Pepper shrugged.

*"Lechón!"* the Unadulterated One screamed, pitching a shower of tulips into his face and slamming the door.

That had happened a year before and Linda still refused to talk to him. It had given Pepper's blues shouts a particularly soulful quality, especially since he continued to preface them, in the style of Screamin' Jay Hawkins, with the words "I love you." *I love you! Aiiyyaaaaaa!!!*

Pepper even had Screamin' Jay's blues snork down.

We'd stand at the shadowy mouth of the viaduct, peering at the greenish gleam of light at the other end of the tunnel. The green was the grass and trees of Douglas Park. Pepper would begin slamming an aerial or board or chain off the girders, making the echoes collide and ring, while Ziggy and I clonked empty bottles and beer cans, and all three of us would be shouting and screaming like Screamin' Jay or Howlin' Wolf, like those choirs of unleashed voices we'd hear on "Jam with Sam's" late-night blues show. Sometimes a train streamed by, booming overhead like part of the song, and we'd shout louder yet, and I'd remember my father telling me how he could have been an opera singer if he hadn't ruined his voice as a kid imitating trains. Once, a gang of black kids appeared on the Douglas Park end of the viaduct and stood harmonizing from bass through falsetto just like the Coasters, so sweetly that though at first we tried outshouting them, we finally shut up and listened, except for Pepper keeping the beat.

We applauded from our side but stayed where we

were, and they stayed on theirs. Douglas Park had become the new boundary after the riots the summer before.

"How can a place with such good viaducts have blight, man?" Pepper asked, still rapping his aerial as we walked back.

"Frankly, man," Ziggy said, "I always suspected it was a little fucked up around here."

"Well, that's different," Pepper said. "Then let them call it an Official Fucked-Up Neighborhood."

Nobody pointed out that you'd never hear a term like that from a public official, at least not in public, and especially not from the office of the mayor who had once promised, "We shall reach new platitudes of success."

Nor did anyone need to explain that Official Blight was the language of revenue, forms in quintuplicate, grants, and federal aid channeled through the Machine and processed with the help of grafters, skimmers, wheeler-dealers, an army of aldermen, precinct captains, patronage workers, their relatives and friends. No one said it, but instinctively we knew we'd never see a nickel.

Not that we cared. They couldn't touch us if we didn't. Besides, we weren't blamers. Blight was just something that happened, like acne or old age. Maybe declaring it official mattered in that mystical world of property values, but it wasn't a radical step, like condemning buildings or labeling a place a slum. Slums were on the other side of the viaduct.

Blight, in fact, could be considered a kind of official recognition, a grudging admission that among blocks of factories, railroad tracks, truck docks, industrial dumps, scrapyards, expressways, and the drainage canal, people had managed to wedge in their everyday lives.

Deep down we believed what Pepper had been getting at: blight had nothing to do with ecstasy. They could send in the building inspectors and social workers, the mayor could drive through in his black limo, but they'd never know about the music of viaducts, or churches where saints winked and nodded, or how right next door to me our guitar player, Joey "Deejo" DeCampo, had finally found his title, and inspired by it had begun the Great American Novel, *Blight*, which opened: "The dawn rises like sick old men playing on the rooftops in their underwear."

We had him read that to us again and again.

Ecstatic, Deejo rushed home and wrote all night. I could always tell when he was writing. It wasn't just the wild, dreamy look that overcame him. Deejo wrote to music, usually the 1812 Overture, and since only a narrow gangway between buildings separated his window from mine, when I heard bells and cannon blasts at two in the morning I knew he was creating.

Next morning, bleary-eyed, sucking a pinched Lucky, Deejo read us the second sentence. It ran twenty ballpoint-scribbled loose-leaf pages and had nothing to do with the old men on the rooftops in their underwear. It seemed as though Deejo had launched into a digression before the novel had even begun. His second sentence described an epic battle between a spider and a caterpillar. The battle took place in the gangway between our apartment buildings, and that's where Deej insisted on reading it to us. The gangway lent his voice an echoey ring. He read with his eyes glued to the page, his free hand gesticulat-

ing wildly, pouncing spiderlike, fingers jabbing like a
beak tearing into green caterpillar guts, fist opening like
a jaw emitting shrieks. His voice rose as the caterpillar
reared, howling like a damned soul, its poisonous hairs
bristling. Pepper, Ziggy, and I listened, occasionally
exchanging looks.

It wasn't Deejo's digressing that bothered us. That
was how we all told stories. But we could see that
Deejo's inordinate fascination with bugs was surfacing
again. Not that he was alone in that, either. Of all our
indigenous wildlife—sparrows, pigeons, mice, rats, dogs,
cats—it was only bugs that suggested the grotesque
richness of nature. A lot of kids had, at one time or
another, expressed their wonder by torturing them a
little. But Deejo had been obsessed. He'd become diaboli-
cally adept as a destroyer, the kind of kid who would
observe an ant hole for hours, even bait it with a Holloway
bar, before blowing it up with a cherry bomb. Then one
day his grandpa Tony said, "Hey, Joey, pretty soon
they're gonna invent little microphones and you'll be
able to hear them screaming."

He was kidding, but the remark altered Deejo's
entire way of looking at things. The world suddenly
became one of an infinite number of infinitesimal voices,
and Deejo equated voices with souls. If one only listened,
it was possible to hear tiny choirs that hummed at all
hours as on a summer night, voices speaking a language
of terror and beauty that, for the first time, Deejo
understood.

It was that vision that turned him into a poet, and
it was really for his poetry, more than his guitar playing, that we'd recruited him for the No Names. None

of us could write lyrics, though I'd tried a few take-offs, like the one on Jerry Lee Lewis's "Great Balls of Fire":

> My BVDs were made of thatch,
> You came along and lit the match,
> I screamed in pain, my screams grew higher,
> Goodness gracious! My balls were on fire!

We were looking for a little more soul, words that would suggest Pepper's rages, Ziggy's prophetic dreams. And we might have had that if Deejo could have written a bridge. He'd get in a groove like "Lonely Is the Falling Rain":

> Lonely is the falling rain,
> Every drop
> Tastes the same,
> Lonely is the willow tree,
> Green dress draped
> Across her knee,
> Lonely is the boat at sea . . .

Deejo could go on listing lonely things for pages, but he'd never arrive at a bridge. His songs refused to circle back on themselves. They'd just go on and were impossible to memorize.

He couldn't spell, either, which never bothered us but created a real problem when Pepper asked him to write something that Pepper could send to Linda Molina. Deejo came up with "I Dream," which, after several pages, ended with the lines:

*I dream of my arms*
*Around your waste.*

Linda mailed it back to Pepper with those lines circled and in angry slashes of eyebrow pencil the exclamations: *!Lechón! !!Estúpido!! !Pervert!*

Pepper kept it folded in his wallet like a love letter.

But back to *Blight*.

We stood in the gangway listening to Deejo read. His seemingly nonstop sentence was reaching a climax. Just when the spider and caterpillar realized their battle was futile, that neither could win, a sparrow swooped down and gobbled them both up.

It was a parable. Who knows how many insect lives had been sacrificed in order for Deejo to have finally arrived at that moral?

We hung our heads and muttered, "Yeah, great stuff, Deej, that was good, man, no shit, keep it up, be a best-seller."

He folded his loose-leaf papers, stuffed them into his back pocket, and walked away without saying anything.

Later, whenever someone would bring up his novel, *Blight*, and its great opening line, Deejo would always say, "Yeah, and it's been all downhill from there."

As long as it didn't look as if Deejo would be using his title in the near future, we decided to appropriate it for the band. We considered several variations—Boys from Blight, Blights Out, the Blight Brigade. We wanted to call ourselves Pepper and the Blighters, but Pepper said no way, so we settled on just plain Blighters. That had a lot better ring to it than calling ourselves the No

Names. We had liked being the No Names at first, but it had started to seem like an advertisement for an identity crisis. The No Names sounded too much like one of the tavern-sponsored softball teams the guys back from Korea had formed. Those guys had been our heroes when we were little kids. They had seemed like legends to us as they gunned around the block on Indians and Harleys while we walked home from grade school. Now they hung out at corner taverns, working on beer bellies, and played softball a couple of nights a week on teams that lacked both uniforms and names. Some of their teams had jerseys with the name of the bar that sponsored them across the back, but the bars themselves were mainly named after beers—the Fox Head 400 on Twenty-fifth Street, or the Edelweiss Tap on Twenty-sixth, or down from that the Carta Blanca. Sometimes, in the evenings, we'd walk over to Lawndale Park and watch one of the tavern teams play softball under the lights. Invariably some team calling itself the Damon Demons or the Latin Cobras, decked out in gold-and-black uniforms, would beat their butts.

There seemed to be some unspoken relationship between being nameless and being a loser. Watching the guys from Korea after their ball games as they hung around under the buzzing neon signs of their taverns, guzzling beers and flipping the softball, I got the strange feeling that they had actually chosen anonymity and the loserhood that went with it. It was something they looked for in one another, that held them together. It was as if Korea had confirmed the choice in them, but it had been there before they'd been drafted. I could still remember how they once organized a motorcycle club.

They called it the Motorcycle Club. Actually, nobody even called it that. It was the only nameless motorcycle gang I'd ever heard of.

A lot of those guys had grown up in the housing project that Pepper and Ziggy lived in, sprawling blocks of row houses known simply as "the projects," rather than something ominous sounding like Cabrini-Green. Generations of nameless gangs had roamed the projects, then disappeared, leaving behind odd, anonymous graffiti —unsigned warnings, threats, and imprecations without the authority of a gang name behind them.

It wasn't until we became Blighters that we began to recognize the obscurity that surrounded us. Other neighborhoods at least had identities, like Back of the Yards, Marquette Park, Logan Square, Greektown. There were places named after famous intersections, like Halsted and Taylor. Everyone knew the mayor still lived where he'd been born, in Bridgeport, the neighborhood around Sox Park. We heard our area referred to sometimes as Zone 8, after its postal code, but that never caught on. Nobody said, "Back to Zone 8." For a while Deejo had considered *Zone* 8 as a possible title for his novel, but he finally rejected it as sounding too much like science fiction.

As Blighters, just walking the streets we became suddenly aware of familiar things we didn't have names for, like the trees we'd grown up walking past, or the flowers we'd always admired that bloomed around the blue plastic shrine of the Virgin in the front yard of the Old Widow. Even the street names were mainly numbers, something I'd never have noticed if Debbie Weiss, a girl I'd met downtown, hadn't pointed it out.

Debbie played sax, too, in the band at her all-girls high school. I met her in the sheet-music department of Lyon & Healy's music store. We were both flipping through the same Little Richard songbooks. His songs had great sax breaks, the kind where you roll onto your back and kick your feet in the air while playing.

"Tenor or alto?" she asked without looking up from the music.

I glanced around to make sure she was talking to me. She was humming "Tutti Frutti" under her breath.

"Tenor," I answered, amazed we were talking.

"That's what I want for my birthday. I've got an alto, an old Martin. It was my uncle Seymour's. He played with Chick Webb."

"Oh, yeah," I said, impressed, though I didn't know exactly who Chick Webb was. "How'd you know I played sax?" I asked her, secretly pleased that I obviously looked like someone who did.

"It was either that or you've got weird taste in ties. You always walk around wearing your neck strap?"

"No, I just forgot to take it off after practicing," I explained, effortlessly slipping into my first lie to her. Actually, I had taken to wearing the neck strap for my saxophone sort of in the same way that the Mexican guys in the neighborhood wore gold chains dangling outside their T-shirts, except that instead of a cross at the end of my strap I had a little hook, which looked like a mysterious Greek letter, from which the horn was meant to hang.

We went to a juice bar Debbie knew around the corner from the music store. I had a Coco-Nana and she had something with mango, papaya, and passion fruit.

"So how'd you think I knew you played sax? By your thumb callus?" She laughed.

We compared the thumb calluses we had from holding our horns. She was funny. I'd never met a girl so easy to talk to. We talked about music and saxophone reeds and school. The only thing wrong was that I kept telling her lies. I told her I played in a band in Cicero in a club that was run by the Mafia. She said she'd never been to Cicero, but it sounded like really the pits. "Really the pits" was one of her favorite phrases. She lived on the North Side and invited me to visit. When she wrote her address down on a napkin and asked if I knew how to get there. I said, "Sure, I know where that is."

North to Freedom, I kept thinking on my way to her house the first time, trying to remember all the bull I'd told her. It took over an hour and two transfers to get there. I ended up totally lost. I was used to streets that were numbered, streets that told you exactly where you were and what was coming up next. "Like knowing the latitude," I told her.

She argued that the North Side had more class because the streets had names.

"A number lacks character, David. How can you have a feeling for a street called Twenty-second?" she asked.

She'd never been on the South Side except for a trip to the museum.

I'd ride the Douglas Park B train home from her house and pretend she was sitting next to me, and as my stop approached I'd look down at the tarpaper roofs, back porches, alleys, and backyards crammed between factories and try to imagine how it would look to someone seeing it for the first time.

.   .   .

At night, Twenty-second was a streak of colored lights, electric winks of neon glancing off plate glass and sidewalks as headlights surged by. The air smelled of restaurants—frying burgers, pizza parlors, the cornmeal and hot-oil blast of *taquerías*. Music collided out of open bars. And when it rained and the lights on the oily street shimmered, Deejo would start whistling "Harlem Nocturne" in the backseat.

I'd inherited a '53 Chevy from my father. He hadn't died, but he figured the car had. It was a real Blightmobile, a kind of mustardy, baby-shit yellow where it wasn't rusting out, but built like a tank, and rumbling like one, too. That car would not lay rubber, not even when I'd floor it in neutral, then throw it into drive.

Some nights there would be drag races on Twenty-fifth Place, a dead-end street lined with abandoned factories and junkers that winos dumped along the curb. It was suggested to me more than once that my Chevy should take its rightful place along the curb with the junkers. The dragsters would line up, their machines gleaming, customized, bull-nosed, raked, and chopped, oversize engines revving through chrome pipes; then someone would wave a shirt and they'd explode off, burning rubber down an aisle of wrecks. We'd hang around watching till the cops showed up, then scrape together some gas money and go riding ourselves, me behind the wheel and Ziggy fiddling with the radio, tuning in on the White Sox while everyone else shouted for music.

The Chevy had one customized feature: a wooden bumper. It was something I was forced to add after I almost ruined my life forever on Canal Street. When I first inherited the car all I had was my driver's permit, so Ziggy, who already had his license, rode with me to take the driving test. On the way there, wheeling a corner for practice, I jumped the curb on Canal Street and rumbled down the sidewalk until I hit a NO PARKING sign and sent it flying over the bridge. Shattered headlights showered the windshield and Ziggy was choking on a scream caught in his throat. I swung a U and fled back to the neighborhood. It took blocks before Ziggy was able to breathe again. I felt shaky too and started to laugh with relief. Zig stared at me as if I were crazy and had purposely driven down the sidewalk in order to knock off a NO PARKING sign.

"Holy Christ! Dave, you could have ruined your life back there forever," Zig told me. It sounded like something my father would have said. Worries were making Ziggy more nervous that summer than ever before. The Sox had come from nowhere to lead the league, triggering Zig's old nightmare about atom bombs falling on the night the White Sox won the pennant.

Besides the busted headlights, the sign pole had left a perfect indentation in my bumper. It was Pepper's idea to wind chains around the bumper at the point of indentation, attach the chains to the bars of a basement window, and floor the car in reverse to pull out the dent. When we tried it the bumper tore off. So Pepper, who saw himself as mechanically inclined, wired on a massive wooden bumper. He'd developed a weird affection for the Chevy. I'd let him drive and he'd tool down alleys clipping garbage cans with the wooden front end in a kind of steady bass-drum beat: *boom boom boom.*

Pepper reached the point where he wanted to drive all the time. I understood why. There's a certain feeling of freedom you can get only with a beater, that comes from being able to wreck it without remorse. In a way it's like being indestructible, impervious to pain. We'd cruise the neighborhood on Saturdays, and everywhere we looked guys would be waxing their cars or tinkering under the hoods.

I'd honk at them out the window on my sax and yell, "You're wasting a beautiful day on that hunk of scrap."

They'd glance up from their swirls of simonize and flip me the finger.

"Poor, foolish assholes," Pepper would scoff.

He'd drive with one hand on the wheel and the other smacking the roof in time to whatever was blaring on the radio. The Chevy was like a drum-set accessory to him. He'd jump out at lights and start bopping on the hood. Since he was driving, I started toting along my sax. We'd pull up to a bus stop where people stood waiting in a trance and Pepper would beat on a fender while I wailed a chorus of "Hand Jive"; then we'd jump back in the Chevy and grind off, as if making our getaway. Once the cops pulled us over and frisked us down. They examined my sax as if it were a weapon.

"There some law against playing a little music?" Pepper kept demanding.

"That's right, jack-off," one of the cops told him, "It's called disturbing the peace."

Finally, I sold Pepper the Chevy for twenty-five dollars. He said he wanted to fix it up. Instead, he used it as a battering ram. He drove it at night around construction sites for the new expressway, mowing down the blinking yellow barricades and signs that read: SORRY FOR THE INCONVENIENCE . . .

Ziggy, who had developed an eye twitch and had started to stutter, refused to ride with him anymore.

The Sox kept winning.

One night, as Pepper gunned the engine at a red light on Thirty-ninth, the entire transmission dropped out into the street. He, Deejo, and I pushed the car for blocks and never saw a cop. There was a slight decline to the street and once we got it moving, the Chevy rolled along on its own momentum. Pepper sat inside steering. With the key in the ignition the radio still played.

"Anybody have any idea where we're rolling to?" Deejo wanted to know.

"To the end of the line," Pepper said.

We rattled across a bridge that spanned the drainage canal, and just beyond it Pepper cut the wheel and we turned off onto an oiled, unlighted cinder road that ran past a foundry and continued along the river. The road angled downhill, but it was potholed and rutted and it took all three of us grunting and struggling to keep the car moving.

"It would have been a lot easier to just dump it on Twenty-fifth Place," Deejo panted.

"No way, man," Pepper said. "We ain't winos."

"We got class," I said.

The road was intersected by railroad tracks. After half an hour of rocking and heaving we got the Chevy onto the tracks and from there it was downhill again to the railroad bridge. We stopped halfway across the bridge. Pepper climbed onto the roof of the car and looked out

over the black river. The moon shined on the oily surface like a single, intense spotlight. Frankie Avalon was
singing on the radio.

"Turn that simp off. I hate him," Pepper yelled. He
was peeing down onto the hood in a final benediction.

I switched the radio dial over to the late-night mush-
music station—Sinatra singing "These Foolish Things"
—and turned the volume up full blast. Pepper jumped
down, flicked the headlights on, and we shoved the car
over the bridge.

The splash shook the girders. Pigeons crashed out
from under the bridge and swept around confusedly in
the dark. We stared over the side half expecting to see
the Chevy bob back up through the heavy grease of the
river and float off in the moonlight. But except for the
bubbles on the surface, it was gone. Then I remembered
that my sax had been in the trunk.

A week later, Pepper had a new car, a red Fury convertible.
His older cousin Carmen had cosigned. Pepper had made
the first payment, the only one he figured on making,
by selling his massive red-sparkle drum set—bass, snare,
tom-tom, cymbals, high hat, bongos, conga, cowbell,
woodblock, tambourine, gong—pieces he'd been accumu-
lating on birthdays, Christmases, confirmation, gradua-
tion, since fourth grade, the way girls add pearls to a
necklace. When he climbed behind those drums, he looked
like a mad king beating his throne, and at first we
refused to believe he had sold it all, or that he was
dropping out of school to join the marines.

He drove the Fury as gently as a chauffeur. It was as
if some of the craziness had drained out of him when the

Chevy went over the bridge. Ziggy even started riding with us again, though every time he'd see a car pass with a GO GO SOX sign he'd get twitchy and depressed.

Pennant fever was in the air. The city long accustomed to losers was poised for a celebration. Driving with the top down brought the excitement of the streets closer. We were part of it. From Pepper's Fury the pace of life around us seemed different, slower than it had from the Chevy. It was as if we were in a speedboat gliding through.

Pepper would glide repeatedly past Linda Molina's house, but she was never out as she'd been the summer before, sunning on a towel on the boulevard grass. There was a rumor that she'd gotten knocked up and had gone to stay with relatives in Texas. Pepper refused to believe it, but the rest of us got the feeling that he had joined the marines for the same reason Frenchmen supposedly joined the foreign legion.

"Dave, man, you wanna go by that broad you know's house on the North Side, man?" he would always offer.

"Nah," I'd say, as if that would be boring.

We'd just drive, usually farther south, sometimes almost to Indiana, where the air smelled singed and towering foundry smokestacks erupted shooting sparks, like gigantic Roman candles. Then, skirting the worst slums, we'd head back through dark neighborhoods broken by strips of neon, the shops grated and padlocked, but bands of kids still out splashing in the water of open hydrants, and guys standing in the light of bar signs, staring hard as we passed.

We toured places we'd always heard about—the Fulton produce mart with its tailgate-high sidewalks,

Midway Airport, skid row—stopped for carryout ribs, or at shrimp houses along the river, and always ended up speeding down the Outer Drive, along the skyline-glazed lake, as if some force had spun us to the inner rim of the city. That was the summer Deejo let his hair get long. He was growing a beard, too, a Vandyke, he called it, though Pepper insisted it was really trimmings from other parts of Deejo's body pasted on with Elmer's glue.

Wind raking his shaggy hair, Deejo would shout passages from his dog-eared copy of *On the Road*, which he walked around reading like a breviary ever since seeing Jack Kerouac on "The Steve Allen Show." I retaliated in a spooky Vincent Price voice, reciting poems off an album called *Word Jazz* that Deej and I had nearly memorized. My favorite was "The Junkman," which began:

> *In a dream I dreamt that was no dream,*
> *In a sleep I slept that was no sleep,*
> *I saw the junkman in his scattered yard . . .*

Ziggy dug that one, too.

By the time we hit downtown and passed Buckingham Fountain with its spraying, multicolored plumes of light, Deejo would be rhapsodic. One night, standing up in the backseat and extending his arms toward the skyscraper we called God's House because of its glowing blue dome—a blue the romantic, lonely shade of runway lights—Deejo blurted out, "I dig beauty!"

Even at the time, it sounded a little extreme. All we'd had were a couple of six-packs. Pepper started swerving, he was laughing so hard, and beating the side of the car with his fist, and for a while it was as if he was back behind the wheel of the Chevy. It even brought Ziggy out of his despair. We rode around the rest of the night gaping and pointing and yelling, "Beauty ahead! Dig it!"

"Beauty to the starboard!"

"Coming up on it fast!"

"Can you dig it?"

"Oh, wow! I am digging it! I'm digging beauty!"

Deejo got pimped pretty bad about it in the neighborhood. A long time after that night, guys would still be asking him, "Digging any beauty lately?" Or introducing him: "This is Deejo. He digs beauty." Or he'd be walking down the street and from a passing car someone would wave, and yell, "Hey, Beauty-Digger!"

The last week before the Fury was repoed, when Pepper would come by to pick us up, he'd always say, "Hey, man, let's go dig some beauty."

A couple of weeks later, on a warm Wednesday night in Cleveland, Gerry Staley came on in relief with the bases loaded in the bottom of the ninth, threw one pitch, a double-play ball, Aparicio to Kluszewski, and the White Sox clinched their first pennant in forty years. Pepper had already left on the bus for Parris Island. He would have liked the celebration. Around 11:00 p.m. the air-raid sirens all over the city began to howl. People ran out into the streets in their bathrobes crying and praying, staring up past the roofs as if trying to catch a glimpse of the mushroom cloud before it blew the neighborhood to smithereens. It turned out that Mayor Daley, a lifelong Sox fan, had ordered the sirens as part of the festivities.

Ziggy wasn't the same after that. He could hardly

get a word out without stammering. He said he didn't feel reprieved but as if he had died. When the sirens started to wail, he had climbed into bed clutching his rosary which he still had from grade-school days, when the Blessed Mother used to smile at him. He'd wet the bed that night and had continued having accidents every night since. Deej and I tried to cheer him up, but what kept him going was a book by Thomas Merton called *The Seven Storey Mountain*, which one of the priests at the parish church had given him. It meant more to Zig than *On the Road* did to Deejo. Finally, Ziggy decided that since he could hardly talk anyway, he might be better off in the Trappists like Thomas Merton. He figured if he just showed up with the book at the monastery in Gethsemane, Kentucky, they'd have to take him in.

"I'll be taking the vow of silence," he stammered, "so don't worry if you don't hear much from me."

"Silence isn't the vow I'd be worrying about," I said, still trying to joke him out of it, but he was past laughing and I was sorry I'd kidded him.

He, Deejo, and I walked past the truck docks and railroad tracks, over to the river. We stopped on the California Avenue Bridge, from which we could see a succession of bridges spanning the river, including the black railroad bridge we had pushed the Chevy over. We'd been walking most of the night, past churches, under viaducts, along the boulevard, as if visiting the landmarks of our childhood. Without a car to ride around in, I felt like a little kid again. It was Zig's last night, and he wanted to walk. In the morning he intended to leave home and hitchhike to Kentucky. I had an image of him standing along the shoulder holding up a sign that read GETHSEMANE to the oncoming traffic. I didn't want him to go. I kept remembering things as we walked along and then not mentioning them, like that dream he'd had about him and me and Little Richard. Little Richard had found religion and been ordained a preacher, I'd read, but I didn't think he had taken the vow of silence. I had a fantasy of all the monks with their hoods up, meditating in total silence, and suddenly Ziggy letting go with an ear-splitting, wild, howling banshee blues shout.

The next morning he really was gone.

Deejo and I waited for a letter, but neither of us heard anything.

"He must have taken the vow of silence as far as writing, too," Deejo figured.

I did get a postcard from Pepper sometime during the winter, a scene of a tropical sunset over the ocean, and scrawled on the back the message "Not diggin' much beauty lately." There was no return address, and since Pepper's parents had divorced and moved out of the projects I couldn't track him down.

There was a lot of moving going on. Deejo moved out after a huge fight with his old man. Deej's father had lined up a production-line job for Deejo at the factory where he'd worked for twenty-three years. When Deej didn't show up for work the first day his father came home in a rage and tried to tear Deejo's beard off. So Deej moved in with his older brother, Sal, who'd just gotten out of the navy and had a bachelor pad near Old Town. The only trouble for Deejo was that he had to move back home on weekends, when Sal needed more privacy.

Deejo was the last of the Blighters still playing. He actually bought a guitar, though not an electric one. He spent a lot of time listening to scratchy old 78s of black singers whose first names all seemed to begin with either Blind or Sonny. Deejo even cut his own record, a paper-thin 45 smelling of acetate, with one side blank. He took copies of it around to all the bars that the guys from Korea used to rule and talked the bartenders into putting his record on the jukebox. Those bars had quieted down. There weren't enough guys from the Korean days still drinking to field the corner softball teams anymore. The guys who had become regulars were in pretty sad shape. They sat around, endlessly discussing baseball and throwing dice for drinks. The jukeboxes that had once blasted The Platters and Buddy Holly had filled up with polkas again and with Mexican songs that sounded suspiciously like polkas. Deejo's record was usually stuck between Frank Sinatra and Ray Charles. Deej would insert a little card handprinted in ballpoint pen: HARD-HEARTED WOMAN BY JOEY DECAMPO.

It was a song he'd written. Deejo's hair was longer than ever, his Vandyke had filled in, and he'd taken to wearing sunglasses and huaraches. Sometimes he would show up with one of the girls from Loop Junior College, which was where he was going to school. He'd bring her into the Edelweiss or the Carta Blanca, usually a wispy blonde with scared eyes, and order a couple of drafts. The bartender or one of us at the bar would pick up Deejo's cue and say, "Hey, how about playing that R5?" and feed the jukebox. "Hard-hearted Woman" would come thumping out as loud as the "She's-Too-Fat Polka," scratchy as an old 78, Deejo whining through his nose, strumming his three chords.

> *Hard-hearted woman,*
> *Oh yeah, Lord,*
> *She's a hard-hearted woman,*
> *Uuuhhh . . .*

Suddenly, despite the Delta accent, it would dawn on the girl that it was Deejo's voice. He'd kind of grin, shyly admitting that it was, his fingers on the bar tapping along in time with the song, and I wondered what she would think if she could have heard the one I wished he had recorded, the one that opened:

> *The dawn rises,*
> *Uuuhhh,*
> *Like sick old men,*
> *Oh, Lord,*
> *Playing on the rooftops in their underwear,*
> *Yeah . . .*

Back to blight.

It was a saying that faded from my vocabulary, especially after my parents moved to Berwyn. Then, some years later, after I quit my job at UPS in order to hide out from the draft in college, the word resurfaced in an English-lit survey class. Maybe I was just more attuned to it than most people ordinarily would be. There seemed to be blight all through Dickens and Blake. The class was taught by a professor nicknamed "the Spitter." He loved to read aloud, and after the first time, nobody sat in the front rows. He had acquired an Oxford accent, but the more excitedly he read and spit, the more I could detect the South Side of Chicago underneath the veneer, as if his *th*'s had been worked over with a drill press. When he read us Shelley's "To a Skylark," which began "Hail to thee, blithe spirit," I thought he was talking about blight again until I looked it up.

One afternoon in spring I cut class and rode the Douglas Park B back. It wasn't anything I planned. I just wanted to go somewhere and think. The draft board was getting ready to reclassify me and I needed to figure out why I felt like telling them to get rammed rather than just saying the hell with it and doing what they told me to do. But instead of thinking, I ended up remembering my early trips back from the North Side, when I used to pretend that Debbie Weiss was riding with me, and when I came to my stop on Twenty-second Street this time it was easier to imagine how it would have looked to her—small, surprisingly small in the way one is surprised returning to an old grade-school classroom.

I hadn't been back for a couple of years. The neighborhood was mostly Mexican now, with many of the signs over the stores in Spanish, but the bars were still called the Edelweiss Tap and the Budweiser Lounge. Deejo and I had lost touch, but I heard that he'd been drafted. I made the rounds of some of the bars looking for his song on the jukeboxes, but when I couldn't find it even in the Carta Blanca, where nothing else had changed, I gave up. I was sitting in the Carta Blanca having a last, cold *cerveza* before heading back, listening to "CuCuRuCuCu Paloma" on the jukebox and watching the sunlight streak in through the dusty wooden blinds. Then the jukebox stopped playing, and through the open door I could hear the bells from three different churches tolling the hour. They didn't quite agree on the precise moment. Their rings overlapped and echoed one another. The streets were empty, no one home from work or school yet, and something about the overlapping of those bells made me remember how many times I'd had dreams, not prophetic ones like Ziggy's, but terrifying all the same, in which I was back in my neighborhood, but lost, everything at once familiar and strange, and I knew if I tried to run, my feet would be like lead, and if I stepped off a curb, I'd drop through space, and then in the dream I would come to a corner that would feel so timeless and peaceful, like the Carta Blanca with the bells fading and the sunlight streaking through, that for a moment it would feel as if I'd wandered into an Official Blithe Area.

# OUTTAKES

The usher scans the credits for his name.

His profession is a hush.

But someday the story will be a legend: how he was discovered, just an ordinary kid off the streets, watching a factory burn down. It was the theater manager who spotted him in that nearly faceless crowd of gapers that disasters assemble. It was the theater manager who later explained to him that out of all the spectators he was the only one with the haloed profile of a pyromaniac, that in a black-and-white night the flames had played technicolor on his face.

He didn't mention it to the theater manager then, but he wasn't used to people speaking to him quite so dramatically.

"I think you got that something special, kid. Come down to the theater tomorrow, 11:00 a.m. sharp. You'll start the matinee."

That was it. It was that simple.

"You like Bugs Bunny, kid?"

"Yeah, I like Bugs."

"Bugs, huh, first-name basis, huh? I like your brass, kid. You're gonna do just fine."

They gave him a flashlight that glowed like an electric rose. Opened the usher's wardrobe to him, where the maroon uniform hung: an epauleted jacket with gold braid like something Brando might wear as Mr. Christian. So he became first mate in the navy of night. Him, the kid who watched fires as if he set them, whose other costumes had been altar boy, newspaper boy, and all-American boy as Mickey Rooney might have played it.

They taught him to tread softly on popcorn, to become a shadow as transparent as sound-track music so that his corporeal body never eclipsed the projectionist's beam.

They taught him how to slide among lovers, taught him the swan dive—a daredevil merger of Fred Astaire and Tarzan—from the balcony over the audience of dreamers dreaming their one dream, taught him to glide above their trance searching for an empty seat.

So he became nocturnal, a member of a secret society that knew itself exiled from the screen, but like outtakes remained part of the movie.

# BIJOU

The film that rumor has made the dernier cri of this year's festival is finally screened.

It begins without credits, challenging the audience from its opening frame. Not only has it been shot in black and white, but the black and white do not occur in usual relationships to one another. There is little gray. Ordinary light has become exotic as zebras.

Perhaps in the film's native country they are not familiar with abstract reductions such as black and white. There, even vanilla ice cream is robin's-egg blue, and licorice almost amethyst when held to the sun. No matter what oppressive regime, each day vibrates with the anima of primitive paintings—continual fiesta! As ambulances siren, they flash through color changes with the rapidity of chameleons. In the modern hospital, set like a glass mural against the sea, ceiling fans oscillate like impaled wings of flamingos above the crisp rhythm of nurses.

Black and white are not native to these latitudes. And gray requires the opaque atmosphere of Antwerp or Newcastle, Pittsburgh or Vladivostok, requires the industrial revolution, laissez-faire, imperialism, Seven Year Plan, Great Leap Forward, pollution, cold war, fallout, PCB, alienation. . . .

Nor does the film appear to be alluding to the classic black-and-white films of Fritz Lang, King Vidor, Orson Welles. Nor to the social realism of the forties or neo-realism of the fifties. In fact, the only acknowledged influence is an indirect one, that of an obscure poem by Victor Guzman, the late surrealist dentist of Chilpancingo.

Trees, for example, are blinding white, rather than the darknesses so often etched against a dying sky.

Shade is white.

Fruit is white.

Asphalt roads are white.

It is the windowpanes through which one sees them that are black. Smoked with kerosene or smeared with shoe polish for secrecy or air-raid blackouts, who can determine?

It is true that at times the film closely resembles a negative—the moon a sooty zero in a silver nitrate night. But the gimmick of shooting in negative is used with restraint. It's obvious that the filmmakers are after something beyond the simple reversal of the values of light.

Take the clouds—plumed, milky black in an albino, noon sky. But are they clouds? Or the smoke from a burning village, bombs, an erupting volcano?

In another sequence, an execution, there is a close-up of bullets being x'd to make the heads dumdum. The

lead is white. And later, when the flour sack hoods are
removed from the prisoners, the wounds are white. The
camera pans along the riddled convent wall. In the
distance, mountains rise tipped with anthracite. To put
it another way, black is not meant to define white, nor
vice versa.

The first color goes almost unnoticed.

The pink washrag of a cat's tongue as it grooms in
the bleached shadow of the jail.

Almost unnoticed—but a subconscious shock regis-
ters through the theater.

Gradually, it becomes apparent that tongues, only
tongues, are assuming color: dogs panting in the dust of
traffic, snakes and geckos flicking from drainpipes, color
licking and poking from a thousand tiny caves.

Even tongues ordinarily colorless take on brilliance:
the black lash of the butterfly uncoils azure at the flower;
the cow masticating its cud lolls a tongue suddenly
crimson as black jeeps siren past down the alabaster
highway to the interior.

There, the guerrillas have been ambushed, surrounded,
betrayed. A chopper flattens palms as it drops in CIA
advisers. The camera pans the faces of the rebels in
macro lens close-ups as if a boil or a louse swelling
among beads of sweat might reveal a man's character; or
as if white hairs sprouting from a mole, or a childhood
scar beneath a stubble beard might tell his past.

And it is here that the tongues begin to obsess the
camera, that the realistic soundtrack of bird caws,
gunshots, shouting, machinery, is intercut with the
whispered litany of Guzman's lines from *Laughing Gas*:
*gold-dust tongues, ocher tongues eating earth, walking*

*tongue, candy tongue, milky tongue, sleeper's tongue, passion's tongues, cankered tongues, tongues tinctured yellow, flaming tongue, hovering tongues of epiphany . . .*

The screen is nearly technicolor with tongues.

Canisters of nerve gas explode.

Then, in a sequence more excruciating than any since *The Battle of Algiers*, the guerrillas are captured. Scene follows scene documenting torture in the modern military state. Cattle prods are used for confessions, electrodes taped to eyelids, tongues, genitals.

At night, out by the black fire, the guards have begun to drink. Soon they cannot tolerate the refined torments of electricity. Fists, truncheons, empty bottles, boots pummel bone.

The prisoners refuse to talk.

Near dawn, in a drunken rage, the guards take them one by one and mock their silence by tearing out their tongues with wire snips. They are forced to kneel, mouths wedged open with a wooden stake, and tongues forceped out in a scream and dark gush of blood—blue, green, yellow, orange, violet, red tongues. The tongues are collected in a coffee can the way ears are sometimes collected, and stored on the colonel's desk. Each new victim stares at the can as he is questioned for the final time. The tongues brim over and flop to the floor and the guards pass out from drunkenness, their own tongues gaping from snoring jaws.

"Raspberry tongues," Guzman wrote, "the entrails of a clown."

The audience stares in silence. Some have turned away; there have been gasps. But, on the whole, they have been conditioned to accept, almost to expect, this violence on screen. They have watched blood spurt and limbs dismembered in Peckinpah's choreographed slow motion, brains sprayed across a wall, bodies explode, monks topple in flaming gasoline, eyes gouged, chain saws buzzing through bone, decapitations in 3-D. They are not at the festival to censor but to discern: where is violence statement and where merely further exploitation? When does Art become carnography? Is this perhaps the Cinema of Cruelty?

They watch as the next morning a young private is assigned to clean up the night's excesses. He takes the coffee can to bury in the old graveyard behind the cathedral while bells chime through an intermittent hiss of wind and mewing of gulls. His shovel bites dirt and he breathes louder with every scoopful he flings over his shoulder into the blurred eye of climbing sun. He sweats, his breath becomes panting, then gagging, and suddenly he's doubled over retching into the hole, mumbling the Lord's Prayer in between spasms. Still heaving, he rises, kicks the can in, frantically raking over loose dirt, smacking it down with the flat of the shovel, raining down blows as if he were killing a snake.

The sound track cuts off.

The whump of the shovel is the last sound, though on screen the soldier continues to beat the earth.

Now the screen seems even more unrelievedly black and white—no more background strumming of guitars, no mountain flutes, birdcalls, wind, distant thunder of gunfire. Not even the unavoidable drone of a jet over-head on its way to another country. A world of action suddenly mute as Griffith's galloping Klan, as Méliès blasting off for the moon, as Chaplin twirling a cane.

There is only the faint, nearly subliminal metronome of ticking sprockets audible from the projection booth in the now-silent theater. But as the silence continues, the steady clack seems increasingly obtrusive, and the suspicion begins to arise that the racket of sprockets *is* the sound track. There's something too rickety about its clatter—a sound that evokes, perhaps by design, evenings long ago, when after the supper dishes were cleared, a father, who served as director, would set up a projector with tinny spools while children removed pictures from a wall to transform it into a screen, and then the lights would be extinguished and home movies would beam into unsteady focus—silent, unedited, the mugging face of each family member plainer than memory, appearing as they once were, startlingly young, innocent of time.

Subtitles begin to appear. Too fast to read. Partially telegraphed messages. Single words or parts of words flashed on screen: AWE DIS KER.

Static as the words, a progression of freeze-frames, the bled tones of tabloid photos dissolve one into another: peasants on their way to market, slum children, children with rickets, a beggar with yaws, fruit loaders sweating at an outdoor market of gutted fish, piled monkey skulls, tourists.

In churches and universities, on corners beneath bug-clouded lights, people are opening their mouths to speak, but everywhere it appears the mouths are black, gaping holes. There is only continual silence, intercut dissolves, subtitles flashing on and off, sometimes like fading neon signs, sometimes like a collage, commenting on the action (WHERE THERE IS NO FREEDOM WORDS FILL THE MOUTH WITH BLOOD).

The footage continues running faster, almost blurred, as if a documentary were being filmed from a speeding train—assassinations, bombed motorcades, bombed restaurants, bombed schools, strikes, soldiers firing into a crowd, smoldering bodies, mothers in mourning, black coffins, black flags, the revolt of students, the revolt of the army, newspaper offices ransacked by Blackshirts, presses smashed, mobs, fires, men hauled out into the street and lynched from lampposts before the shattered windows of the capitol, streets littered with books from the gutted library, and all the while a sound rising from underground as if the clatter of sprockets has become a subway train roaring down a tunnel, its brake shoe scraping metal from track, metal on metal whining into a siren-pitched screech (EVEN THE HANGED HAVE NO TONGUES TO PROTRUDE!).

The house lights flick on. The audience, many of them North Americans, is stunned. Some talk as if making sure they still can. Some weep. Others leave the theater cursing—what? The film? The oppressors? It isn't clear. Someone in the balcony shouts, "Bravo!" And another in front, "Long live the revolution!" People are up from their seats and applauding as if it were a live presentation.

"The ultimate praise for a film," one critic is heard to remark on his way to the lobby, "is to treat it as if it were a play deserving curtain calls, to confuse celluloid images with flesh and blood, to transcend the isolated private dream state of the movie theater by merging with the mass in simple applause."

Tomorrow the Arts sections will carry rave reviews:

*"a new and daring fusion of avant-garde technique with
documentary sensibility . . . "*

A journalist for the *Voice* will write: "Uncompro-
misingly powerful, it demands to be seen, though a film
like this might be better kept secret, protected from the
corrupting influence of the Hollywood glamour and
promotion machine, the invidious American penchant
for reducing substance to marketable style."

While another reviewer, writing for a more conserva-
tive publication will comment: "This looks like the year
for Terrorist Cinema. Another fad pretending to usher in
a change of consciousness but lacking the moral impera-
tive of the civil rights movement and peace marches that
launched the 60s."

The audience files out through the mirrored lobby,
backs turned on the posters of stars, out under the
winking marquee, squinting at the pink smolder of dusk.
Behind them, on the silver screen in the houselit theater,
a final frame hovers like the ghost image phenomena
sometimes haunting TV screens, a blown-up image that
could only have been shot by a camera implanted in
a mouth, of an indigo tongue working at a husk of
popcorn stuck in a gold-capped molar.

And across this image a delayed rolling of credits
begins: the names of actors, writers, cameramen, assis-
tant director, director, producer, editors, sound, music,
makeup, gaffers, soldiers, officers, generals, politicians—
a cast of thousands—workers, students, peasants, the
audience, the victims, the maimed, the maddened, the
myriad names of the dead.

# STRAYS

Her hands were always scratched from sparring with cats.

I used to watch her out walking some mutt she said she'd found the same way she'd found men.

For years she'd open her house to whatever stray showed up. She never caged them, let them wander in and out of her life—dogs, cats, rabbits, birds. . . .

It seemed she was constantly nursing some kind of bird. Convalescent pigeons would return, roosting and cooing in the eaves above the doorstep where she sprinkled hard corn.

"The starlings never live," she said, "you can't cure a starling."

There would be saucers everywhere, some stained with milk, others brimming with dirty rainwater. She believed in the curative powers of rain.

"I never give any of them names. We don't know an animal's name. A name's what we use instead of smelling."

# NIGHTHAWKS

## SILHOUETTES

The alley became a river in the rain—a river with currents of clattering cans and a floe of cardboard. The boy would wake to the headlights of lightning spraying the walls of his small room, and lie listening to the single note of drops pinging the metal hood of a blue bulb that glowed above a garage door. Finally, he'd go to the window and look down.

The blue bulb gave the rain a bluish gleam. Rotted drainpipes gushed like dislocated fountains. Flooded tar roofs seemed to tilt, spilling waterfalls through sluices of fire escapes.

At the mouth of the alley, a streetlight swirled, slowly disappearing down the whirlpool of a sewer. And beyond the aura of the streetlight, on a street whose name and numbers had been washed away, shadows moved aimlessly through rain. Tonight, they had their collars raised. He could catch glimpses of them passing by the mouth of the alley. Even when he couldn't see them, he could sense their presence: shapes that he'd named *silhouettes*, shadows that threw shadows, that inhabited the hourless times of night stolen from dreams when it seemed to the boy as if he'd been summoned awake only to lie there wondering for what reason he'd been summoned. He couldn't remember when he'd become aware of their presence, or when he first thought of them as silhouettes. He had never thought of them as anything else—not ghosts, or spirits. Silhouettes were enough to haunt him.

Others had their own names for shadows. Downstairs, the Ukrainian kid who practiced the violin slept with his arms extended in the shape of a cross to ward off the dead. Across the alley, in a basement flat, a Puerto Rican girl prayed as if begging before a vigil candle flickering the picture of the Virgin on her bureau, and sometimes the smell of the coal furnace behind the grate that opened on purgatory would fade into a faint scent of roses. There were guys who carried knives taped inside their socks to school, who still slept at the edges of their beds in order to leave room for their guardian angels. There were girls who wore mascara like a mask, who swore they'd seen Niña, the beautiful high school girl who had plunged from a roof one summer night. Niña had sneaked out that night to meet her boyfriend, Choco, a kid who played the conga and had gone AWOL to see her. Choco, his conga drum strapped over his shoulder, had led her up a fire escape to the roof where he slept on an old mattress. They took angel dust, which made the moon seem near enough to step onto from the roof. The girls said that on moonlit nights music would wake them—a song whose beat they all recognized, though none of them could hum back its melody—and they would see a *fantasma*, Niña, her hair flying and blouse billowing open, falling past their windows, but falling so slowly that it seemed as if it might take forever for her to hit the street.

And there were apparitions in broad daylight: the mute knifesharpener pushing his screeching whetstone up alleys; the peddlers with clothesline whips flicking blindered horses as their wagons rumbled by tottering under jumbled loads of uprooted cellars and toppled attics; the hunchbacked woman who walked bent from the waist as if doubled over by the weight of the lifetime's length of filthy, gray hair that streamed from her bowed head and swept the pavement before her.

They seemed part of the streets. If anyone noticed, it was only to glance away, but the boy secretly regarded them as if he were witnessing refugees from a cruel fairy tale groping their way through the ordinary world. He wondered where they disappeared to, where they slept at night, and what they dreamed.

Beside the daytime apparitions, the silhouettes seemed nearly invisible, camouflaged by night, shadows who'd broken their connections to whatever had thrown them, and now wandered free, like dreams escaped from dreamers. They emerged from viaducts on nights when viaducts exhaled fog and manhole covers steamed. Where they stood in dripping doorways, they made the doorways darker. When they stepped into the open—shadows, but shadows no longer supported by walls or trailed along pavement—the rain, slanting through the glow of streetlights and shop signs, beaded off them like molten electricity. Oncoming headlights bent around them;

flashes of lightning traced their outlines. The boy could sense them moving along the street and wondered if tonight was the night for which he'd been summoned awake, when the silhouettes would finally come up the alley, past the guardian streetlight now swirling and sinking, and assemble below his window, looking up at his face pressed against the spattered pane, their eyes and mouths opened onto darkness like the centers of guitars.

Love, it's such a night, laced with running water, irreparable, riddled with a million leaks. A night shaped like a shadow thrown by your absence. Every crack trickles, every overhang drips. The screech of night-hawks has been replaced by the splash of rain. The rain falls from the height of streetlights. Each drop contains its own blue bulb.

# LAUGHTER

I knew a girl who laughed in her sleep. She had been in
the States only a year and I wondered if being foreign
didn't have something to do with her laughing that way.
Her eyes were a gold-flecked green more suited to cats,
and ringed with the longest lashes I'd ever seen. In the
right light her half-lowered lashes threw small shadows
across her face. She didn't look American yet. Once I
woke her and asked what was so funny. She seemed
confused and a little embarrassed, and I never asked
her again.

We met at the ice cream factory where I worked the
summer between high school and college. She was the
first girl I was *serious* about. I felt too young to be
serious — a feeling I kept secret.

She kept me a secret from her uncle Tassos.

Her uncle was the one who had brought her over
and got her the job at the ice-cream factory. She worked
on the bar tank line with the other, mostly foreign
women, sitting before a conveyor belt and packing
Popsicles, Fudgsicles, Creamsicles, and Dreamsicles into
freezer cartons. At the end of the day her hands were
stiff with cold and her fingers stained the colors of
whatever flavors had been run.

Her uncle Tassos worked on the ore boats out of
Calumet Harbor. He would be away for two-week runs,
and then off work for five days straight. When he was
back home the only place I would get to see her was at
the factory. I was still living with my parents and began
to feel ashamed for not having my own place to take her.

When Uncle Tassos left with the barges again—as safely off somewhere around Petoskey as if he'd sailed for Peloponnesus—she'd sneak me up to her one-room apartment that overlooked Halsted Street.

It was an old neighborhood that Mayor Daley, despite his campaign promises, was preparing to demolish to make way for a new university. But life went on that summer as it always had—daily newspapers printed in strange alphabets; nuts, cheeses, dried cod sold in the streets; the scent of crushed lemons from the bakery that made lemon ice; Greek music skirling from the restaurant downstairs. And once she'd let me in I wouldn't leave until morning, but sometimes, in the middle of the night, I'd have to get up and pace while the dark room filled with laughter.

# EVERYTHING

A couple of months after he'd married Joan, the phone rang in the middle of the night. The phone was in the kitchen and seemed to ring through the dark apartment like an alarm. He had always been afraid of phone calls at that hour. They triggered a dread in him that something terrible had happened, and he almost believed that if he didn't answer, whatever catastrophe had occurred might be undone by morning. But this time he leapt to answer. It was better to get the news firsthand than to listen to his new wife answer the phone and then break into sobs.

"Hello," he said, trying to sound composed.

"Yellow. Guess who?"

"I know who."

"Guess what?"

"I give."

"I'm tripping on MDA."

"Oh."

" 'Ecstasy,' you know, the 'Love Drug.' Whatsamatter? You don't read *Newsweek* and keep up?"

"My subscription ran out."

"It's a body rush. Incredibly erotic. I'm so horny—climbing the walls."

"Nice of you to call and let me know."

"It heightens memory, too. Hey, I'm still a little nuts about you. Is that Joanie flushing the toilet?"

"Yes."

"She probably wants to know who's on the phone."

"Exactly right."

"That's why you're talking to me in that funny flat voice. So quiet. Not saying my name. You didn't use to be such a monosyllabic type of guy. Well, at least say something."

"Like what?"

"Like what are you wearing? Cute little seersucker pajamas?"

"Look, I should hang up."

"You're supposed to talk people down when they're tripping. I could be in terrible trouble here. Remember that one time we did mushrooms? The night you said I turned into Cleopatra. You said it was the pinnacle."

"We were in college, for chrissake."

"I thought I'd try something like that one more time, you know, like they shout at the end of Basie's 'April in Paris'—'One more time!'—a tribute to the old days. I liked myself better then. Liked you better, too."

"I don't want to be the one to hang up, okay?"

"You never did. Guess what I'm wearing? Guess how I look on the other end of this telephone line. Listen, I'll rub the phone down my body. See if you can hear . . . did you hear anything?"

"No."

"Well, press your ear against the receiver. You didn't hear that? You didn't hear hair? What part of my body do you think you're talking to right now? Say something soft and breathy. Blow warm air into the phone. Pretend you're a mad breather."

"It's late. You should go to sleep."

"Come over."

"I can't."

"Baby, come see me. Tell her it's a buddy with a flat tire."

"I can't."

"Baby, oh baby, baby, baby, baby, I need you so much tonight. Baby, you gotta fix my flat tire."

"It's 3 a.m."

"Please. Don't make me beg. Come over ... we'll do *everything*."

"How many other people have you called besides me?"

"Only one."

# KILLING TIME

Between job interviews, I'd wander around the Art Institute, killing time. The Art Institute was on the park side of Michigan Avenue, across the street from the towering office buildings in which the employment agencies were situated. It felt soothing to drift among the paintings. Several had begun to feel like old friends. Visiting them beat sitting over a lukewarm coffee in some greasy spoon, spending another afternoon studying not only the Want Ads, but the faces of the others at the counter who sat nursing their coffees as they grimly studied the Want Ads too. By now, I spotted their faces everywhere. I'd become aware of an invisible army armed with Want Ads, pounding the pavement, knocking on doors, hoping opportunity would answer. It was an army without the consolation of camaraderie. I'd learned to recognize its unconscious salutes, its uniforms and ranks and outposts—personnel offices, coffee shops, and stands of public phones—from which its lonely campaigns were launched. I'd been looking for a job for over a month and was beginning to feel desperate.

The Art Institute was my base of operations. Its public phones were usually empty, and its restroom was modern and clean with a full-length mirror perfect for last minute inspections before heading out on an interview.

My first couple weeks of job hunting, I'd hung out at the Public Library. Unlike the Art Institute, admission to the library was free. But the longer I'd gone without work, the more an old dread crept back into me: a feeling from high school, a memory of dreary Saturdays when, loaded with note cards for research papers that I was hopelessly behind on, I'd enter the Public Library only to end up wandering around lost, wasting the day. I remembered how, the summer before I'd started high school, my father had insisted that I spend a week at the library researching professions and the biographies of successful tycoons so that I'd have some sense of direction during my high school years and not live up to his nickname for me: The Dreamer. And I recalled how rather than doing what he'd asked, I'd only pretended to go to the library and instead had spent the money he'd given me at movies and record shops. Now, his dire predictions seemed to be coming true. My money was running out; I couldn't find a job. After a week of hanging around the library, I began to recognize the same set of regulars—people who carried their possessions in bags, or wore them all at once, who seemed to be living in the library stacks. Soon, I expected them to begin winking at me, giving me secret greetings I didn't want to recognize.

The public phones in the Public Library were always busy. In the old restrooms fluids pooled on the cracked terrazzo, and the homeless hung around inside, smoking, sometimes washing out their clothes in the plugged sinks. Even on the brightest days I began to notice the gray, gloomy cast of the marble corridors and flights of stairs. The reading rooms, dominated by the glow of green-shaded desk lamps, seemed worn as old railroad stations. There was a smell of musty pulp, of thumbed cloth covers, of too much print. At the long reading tables I could spot the displaced and dispossessed drowsing over enormous tomes or reading aloud to themselves as if engaged in debates with the complete works of Marx and Engels, Spengler, Tolstoy, Schopenhauer, while outside the windows cooing pigeons paced back and forth along the crusted slate ledges.

The Art Institute, by contrast, seemed flooded with light—not merely the light streaming from skylights or the track lights focused on paintings. The paintings themselves appeared to throw an internal light the way that oaks and maples seem aflame in fall, from the inside out. My favorite painters were the Impressionists. On days when it seemed as if I'd never find a job, when I was feeling desperate, I'd stand before their paintings and stare at them until it seemed I could almost step into their world, that if I closed my eyes and then opened them I'd find myself waking under the red coverlet in Van Gogh's *Bedroom at Arles*. I would open my eyes in a room of pastel light to find that one of Degas' dancers, who had been sleeping beside me, had discarded her chemise and was stepping into her morning bath. Or I would awaken already strolling without a care in and out of patches of precise shade, one of the Sunday crowd along the river on the island of *La Grande Jatte*. I wanted to be somewhere else, to be a dark blur waiting to board the Normandy train in the smoke-smudged *Saint-Lazare* station; I wanted a ticket out of my life, to be riding a train whose windows slid past a landscape of grain stacks in winter fields. It might be taking me to the beach of *Saint-Adresse* where the fishing boats have been drawn up onto the sand and a man with a telescope and his daughter by his side looks out to sea, or to *Pourville* where the wind gusts along the cliff walk and a woman opens an orange parasol while white sails hardly taller than the white-capped waves pitch on the blue-green sea.

Yet, I would always end my walk through the paintings, standing before the diner in Edward Hopper's *Nighthawks*. Perhaps I needed its darkness to balance the radiance of the other paintings. It was night in Hopper's painting; the diner illuminated the dark city corner with a stark light it didn't seem capable of throwing on its own. Three customers sat at the counter as if waiting, not for something to begin, but rather to end, and I knew how effortless it would be to open my eyes and find myself waiting there, too.

# INSOMNIA

There is an all-night diner to which, sooner or later, insomniacs find their way. In winter, when snow drifts over curbs, they cross the trampled intersections until they come upon footprints that perfectly fit their shoes and lead them there. On nights like this in summer, the diner's lighted corner draws them to its otherwise dark neighborhood like moths.

They come from all over the city and beyond—from farm towns in Ohio, Iowa, and Indiana, crossing the unlit prairie, arriving at vacant train stations and bus terminals, then making their way toward that illuminated corner as if it's what they left home to find—a joint that asks no questions and never closes, a place to sit awhile for the price of a cup of coffee.

From the size of the two nickel-plated urns, the place must serve a lot of coffee. And yet it looks almost deserted now—only a couple, stretching out the night, at one end of the counter, and Ray, the blond counterman, bending to rinse out a cup, and a guy in a hat sitting alone with his back to the window. It never gets crowded. They file in and out—the night shift, cabbies, drunks, sometimes a cop, loners mostly—there's never telling who might step through the door.

Earlier this evening, when most of the stools were taken, a woman in heels and a summer dress stopped outside and stood peering in as if looking for someone. At least it seemed that way at first, before it became clear that she'd only stopped to fix her makeup in the reflection of the plate glass. There were mostly men at the counter, and they pretended not to watch as she stroked a comb through her hair. She seemed so unconscious of their presence that watching her would have been like spying on a woman before her own bedroom mirror. Yet, though they didn't stare, the men on the other side of the glass wondered about her; they wondered who it was she had stopped to make herself still prettier for, or if she'd just been with someone and was on her way back to someone else. When she stepped away from the window, the reflection of the lipstick she'd applied seemed to remain hovering on the glass like the impression of a kiss. The men in the diner pretended to ignore this too, although in its way the reflected kiss was no less miraculous than the tears rolling down the cheeks of a parish church's plaster Virgin, that crowds will line up for blocks to see. The woman stepped beyond the light of the diner and disappeared down a street of shadowy windows. After a while, the reflected kiss disappeared too—who knows where—simply dissolving into darkness, or perhaps reappearing blocks away on the glass door of a corner phone booth, where an AWOL soldier named Choco, disoriented by grief as if it were a drug, has wedged inside with his conga drum because he has nowhere else to go. He sits dazed, as if waiting for an oracle to call, and doesn't notice the kiss on the glass door among the graffitied lipsticked initials and eyebrow-penciled numbers. And when he begins to beat the booth, his open palm becoming a bloody handprint on cracked glass, the kiss vanishes again. Perhaps the kiss crosses the city, riding the blurred window of a subway, or of a cab running red lights down a boulevard of black glass. . . .

That couple, stretching out the night at the end of the counter, has been in here before. They sit side by side like lovers, and yet there's something detached enough about them so that they could pass for strangers. It might be the way they sit staring ahead rather than looking at each other, or that their hands on the counter-top don't quite touch, but it's passion, not indifference, that is responsible for that. Tonight, at this late hour, they've wandered in feeling empty, a little drained by the mutual obsession that keeps them awake. The insomnia they share is the insomnia of desire. Walking here along deserted streets, they noticed this neighborhood of shad-owy windows was missing a moon, and so they began to make up a moon between them: solid as a cue ball; translucent and webbed with fine cracks, like bone china; cloudy, the bleached white of a bra tumbling in a dryer. Now, under a fluorescence that makes her arms appear too bare and her dress shimmer from rose to salmon to shades of red for which there's no approximation, they've fallen silent. He's smoking. She dreamily studies a match-book from some other place where they sat like this together killing time.

And Ray, he's been working here long enough to seem like part of the decor. The white of his uniform intensifies the lighting. He keeps the coffee urns gleaming and the counter swabbed. The cocky angle of the white paper cap perched on his blond head makes him look like a kid, but he's older than people take him for; friendly, but as much a loner as anyone he serves. Work-ing nights might seem to grant him an immunity from insomnia, but job or not, he's here like the rest of them, awake. What he does during the day is anybody's guess.

He disappears behind one of those shadowed, black, upper-story windows, draws the shade, and the rising sun beats it gold. The restless sound of traffic carries up to him from the street. Perhaps it's something other than insomnia, to lie listening to children yelling as if they've re-created light; to try to dream, but succeed only in remembering; to toss and sweat in a dirty paste of sheets, while the drone of a ball game is gradually replaced by the buzz of a fly—a fly buzzing like the empty frequencies between stations as its shadow grows enormous between the shade and windowpane. Is it insomnia for a man to wad his ears with the cotton from a pill bottle, to mask his eyes with blinders, and press a stale pillow over his head, praying for another day to burn down, so he can wake into another night?

The guy with his back to the window has been sitting there a long time nursing his mug of java. Ray, stooping to rinse out a cup, avoids looking in his direction. There's something about the way the guy's hat shadows his face, about his shoulders, hunched as if braced for another blow, about his eyes plumbing the depths of his coffee, that discourages conversation. It would be like trying to make small talk with a hit man. Besides, the guy has been mumbling to himself, his mouth moving as if chewing something too bitter to swallow. If he's thinking about women, he must be counting up all the times they've cheated on him. If he's thinking about work, he's adding up the brutal ways of saying they're taking your job: *fired, canned, sacked, axed, terminated.* He's dwelling on the *lost* in "lost his job"—*lost*—as if the eight hours of sweat at the heart of each day could be misplaced. Why call it *lost* if it's been taken from you? *Lost* is a lie, and without such lies the streets would be crowded with assassins. But his incessant tallies, his lists of lies and grievances, his roll call of betrayals, have added up to nothing but insomnia. Insomnia is a private score he has, so far, settled only with himself; it's the time he does each night for his own betrayals, his own petty offenses of failure, hard luck, desperation. And insomnia is also the threat of unnamed crimes still more menacing. After dark, he carries it beside his heart, concealed like a weapon.

And finally, what about the empty water glass set on the counter before an empty stool? No tip beside it. Not that anyone but Ray paid any attention to the person who sat there and ordered merely water. Only Ray recognized immediately that a sleepwalker had entered the diner. They wander in occasionally, and Ray has learned to recognize their habits—how they order nothing but water, and never tip. At first, Ray would serve them only what they asked for, but now sometimes he buys them a coffee on the house. He isn't sure himself whether he does it out of kindness or cruelty. He'd like to think it's kindness, that if it were he who was wandering the streets asleep, he'd be grateful to anyone who tried to help. But Ray's not certain. He's heard it can be dangerous to tamper with sleepwalkers, that their souls can leave their bodies, and so Ray always braces for that moment when the steaming coffee first touches their lips and they wake.

The sleepwalker's eyes roll open. He glances around wildly as if he doesn't realize what's happened or even that he is awake. Fluorescence scalds his pupils as the coffee did his lips. The diner seems frozen in the blinding

pop of a flashbulb that refuses to fade—a glare as stark
as the illumination of certain dreams, brighter for being
framed by night. In that paralyzing light, the sleepwalker sees the lovers at the other end of the counter,
with their bleached-out, hawk-featured faces staring
straight ahead as if they're in a trance; and Ray, glancing
away, caught in the act of dunking a cup under the
counter as if disposing of evidence; and the hit man in
the shadowy hat, mumbling to no one. Stunned as he
is, the sleepwalker can feel the paralysis of the diner
drawing him in as if he belongs there too. With a half
spin, he shoves away from the counter, rises from his
stool, and, leaving no tip, staggers for the door. And as
he pushes out, something snaps him fully awake—maybe
the night air, or the slap of a patty hitting the grill, or his
soul returning to him from shadows. He stands outside
the diner, within the perimeter of its aura, and stares
down a street of dark windows, wondering which way
he's come from, which way to go. In the diner's almost
phosphorescent glow, the deserted street looks like pavement might on the moon. Above the roofs, he can see
the moon the lovers at the end of the counter left behind,
no longer newly minted, surrounded by the same aura
as the diner, waiting faithfully like a dog for them to
reemerge. In their absence, it's gone through phases,
diminishing like a stalled traffic light in the rearview
mirror of a taxi. Now it's less than a crescent, less than
a smudged thumbprint of mother-of-pearl—only a shimmer like the glint of neon on the surface of a cup of
black coffee. The bitter taste of coffee still burns his
tongue. He can feel his nerves jumping and his heart
starting to race as if that mere sip in the diner has stoked

him with the stamina of caffeine, and converted him from sleepwalking to insomnia. From somewhere in the sky above the diner, he hears the screech of a single nighthawk, and suddenly he's happy. It seems to him enough to simply be awake like that bird soaring in the darkness that sleepers have abandoned, to be walking away from the lighted corner, down the empty, silent streets they've left to him, whistling as he passes dark windows, not sure where he's going, and in no hurry to find out. It's the middle of the night, and tomorrow seems as if it's still 93 million miles away.

# GOLD COAST

They wake simultaneously in a hotel room on the thirty-seventh floor, neither of them sure of the time, both still a little drunk, a little numb from the silence that has grown between them.

"Look at the sky! Look at the light!" she exclaims.

He's already seen it—how could he not? The enormous bed faces a wall of windows. They've left the drapes open. The wall of windows now seems like a wall of sky, almost indigo, shot with iridescence as if veins of a newly discovered precious mineral have been exposed. It isn't dawn yet. It's still a gradation of night, but night with tomorrow already luminous behind it like the silver behind the glass of a cobalt mirror.

He can see the sky reflected in the windows of all the surrounding buildings that tower up to form the glass cliffs of the gold coast they've drifted to. He knows that every city has such strips, and he distrusts them. No matter how authentically elegant they might appear, he thinks of them as illusory, removed from the real life of cities, as places that are really no place, reflections floating like illuminated scum on the surface of a river. He remembers how, as teenagers, he and a buddy spent their nights exploring the gold coast in the city they'd grown up in, and the mixture of awe and contempt they'd felt toward it.

He no longer feels superior to gold coasts. He wonders how many of his fellow sleepers are sitting up as he is, silently peering out of highrise rooms in which the drapes have been drawn open on tremendous windows, windows for giants, scaled to encompass the winking horizon of the city. He both envies those still sleeping peacefully and pities them for missing this nameless, early sky which he knows already will be more unforgettable than any dawn he's ever seen. He wonders which of those two emotions the future will reveal as the more accurate. Once, shortly after they'd become lovers, she told him, "I'm not sure if meeting you has been the most lucky or unlucky thing that's ever happened to me."

He had laughed.

"I wasn't kidding," she said.

"I know," he said. "I'm only laughing because that's exactly what I was thinking about meeting you."

"See. Maybe that's what happens when it's fate. One always feels what the other is feeling, at the same time, together." She laughed too.

"Kind of emotional telepathy, eh?"

"'Emotional' makes it sound too *glandular*," she said, rolling her eyes, speaking in the teasing way she had that made for private jokes between them. "I'm not talking about something in the *glands;* I'm talking about something in the stars."

Now, beside him in bed, she whispers, "Why did we have to see this together?" It isn't said cruelly. He understands what she means. She means they've seen this unsuspected sky only because of each other; that it's something more between them to remember. And he knows that he doesn't need to answer, that it's as if he's merely overheard her speaking to herself, almost as if he isn't there any longer, as if she's awakened alone, at an unknown hour, along a gold coast.

# TRANSPORT

A kiss crosses the city. It rides a glass streetcar that showers blue, electric sparks along the ghost of a track—a track paved over in childhood—the line that she and her mother used to take downtown.

A kiss crosses the city, revolves through a lobby door into a rainy night, catches a cab along a boulevard of black glass, and, running red lights, dissolves behind the open fans of wiper blades.

Rain spirals colorlessly out of the dark, darkens all it touches and makes it gleam.

Her kiss crosses the city, enters a subway tunnel that descends at this deserted hour like a channel through an underground world. It's timeless there, always night, as if the planet doesn't turn below the street. At the mouth of the station stands a kid who's gone AWOL and now has nowhere else to go, a young conga drummer, a *congacero*, wearing a fatigue jacket and beating his drum. He has the pigeons up past their bedtime doing the mambo. He leaves his cap of small change behind him on the pavement and steps onto an escalator that carries him down in time to the tock of his drum. The more fervently the *congacero* drums, the deeper the escalator conveys him. He has it doing a rumba, a cha-cha-cha, a *guanguanco*, and finally, possessed, unable to fold back upon itself, the escalator becomes a staircase flowing like quicksilver, a shimmering waterfall, an anaconda slithering through the kingdom of sleep. It will transport him deeper than sleep, deeper than dreams, than nightmares, than the nod of junkies, than comas, until he steps off onto the platform where the newly dead, their souls still shaped like their bodies, mill about in confusion, waiting to be taken to their next destination.

"Is anyone in charge here?" the *congacero* asks, the way a foreigner in a city might seek directions. Despite the mob of souls, his voice echoes as if he's called into a void. He drums now to invoke whatever spirit governs this place, a beat so compelling that the arrhythmic dead begin to sway as if they feel the accompaniment of their own hearts again.

"*Iku la tigwa un bai bai,*" he chants over his drumbeat, magic words in an ancient tongue that, he's been taught, will beckon the *iku*, his dead ancestors, who might intercede for him. But the only response is the hollow silence that his drum continues to punctuate.

The loss of the woman he has descended here to find has taught him that eternity is not a presence, but an absence. His drum shapes silence into time, keeping time where there is none to keep. Time is his song and his power. Drafts from the tunnels swirl about him. In spite of the bone-deep dampness, he's begun to sweat. Sweat, impossible here as tears, patters the drumskin that he leans above with his eyes closed and drumming hands nearly invisible.

The dead file by dancing jerkily like marionettes, but he doesn't notice. They stream around him like a rush-hour crowd past a street musician, a musician so absorbed in his intricate rhythms that he's forgotten the street, and worse, has forgotten how dangerous losing one's street sense can be. Possessed by his own drumming, he's become infused with forgetfulness. He has forgotten to drum in supplication to whatever spirit governs this place. He has forgotten to drum for the *iku*. He has forgotten to dedicate his drumming to his patron saint and guardian, Elleggua, whose necklace of sacred cowrie shells he wears under his fatigue jacket, entangled with his dog tags.

It is for Elleggua, the trickster, Master of Doors and Crossroads, that he should be drumming. Instead, he now drums solely for his lost love, the girl, who, legends say, falls endlessly. One of her perfumed, black nylons is knotted around his head like a sweatband. He has refused to allow his longing for her to turn to grief. The rhythm he weaves for her has never been played before—a slap and swipe of fingertips and palms on the drumskin that evokes the sounds their sweating bodies made against one another. Its ebb and flow is like the lilt of a melody.

His drum song is amplified by the tunnels. Its echoes return delayed almost as if someone far off is at last responding. His conga answers its own echoes. His blurred hands pound still faster and the echoes multiply, first, into a trio of sacred *bata* drummers, and then into a corps of drummers. He disperses his drum corps in search of her. Their frenzied drumming reverberates down every tunnel as if time is pulsing through the underground like blood, and finally, still dazed, she steps summoned from shadow.

He leads her back from the underground. She follows each beat of his conga as if retracing the footprints of a complicated dance step. The way they walk to the rhythm makes it look as if their hips are leading them. Death has not disfigured her beauty, and yet she wears her youthfulness like a mask. Beneath it, her eyes seem glazed, gazing inward as if completely self-absorbed in her still new, utter lack of self. She is serene and silent as he's never seen her. What's been done to you already? he wants to cry, but says nothing. Having glanced at her once, he can't look back at her again until they have returned to the world of sunlight and substance—a world where sparrows twitter in the sapling that has insisted on sprouting from the rubble of a vacant lot, and the only shadows are those of green awnings unfurled above stands of fruits and flowers.

Even in high heels, she floats so lightly that her footfalls aren't audible above the scurrying of rats. Yet, he can't look back to be sure she is following, perhaps because with each step her renunciation of death makes her more terrifyingly beautiful. Or perhaps he doesn't dare to meet her inwardly gazing eyes for fear they will distract him from the steady, urgent domination of his beat. If his faith in his power to keep time here in the confines of eternity is shaken and his beat disrupted for even a moment they will both be lost.

Think only of light, little dove, he wishes to tell her. Open your memory as if you've just awakened and are slowly drawing a window shade up on noon. You'll return to who you were that moment when I first saw you standing in a doorway, sunlight streaming through your dress, illuminating your legs, the lace petals of your underclothes. In broad daylight, I could see the shadows of your breasts as if my eyes had special power.

But when they reach the knot of tunnels, the confluence of steel and slime where subway track and sewers interconnect, he stops. Still drumming, he stands otherwise motionless at the junction where sinkholes bottom out, and dry wells, abandoned mine shafts, and caverns intersect, then burrow off in all directions. The corridors are dark, a labyrinth of catacombs dropping into chasms and black canyons. His drumbeats collide with blind alleys and dead ends, and the cacophony of so many ricocheting echoes overwhelms him. Suddenly, his hands are confused; he's not aware at first, that they've dropped silently to his sides. The drumming continues without him—incessant, chaotic, shattering time rather than keeping it. Where is his guardian, Elleggua, Master of Crossroads, who should have been his guide? If one's patron saint is a trickster, must his blessing be a trick? He looks back to tell her he's lost, but she's no longer there behind him. And when he turns again, she is standing before him as if she has been leading them, as if she is the one who has led them here. He follows her now, his drum dragging behind him, his eyes on her back as they move off deeper into the twisting passageways. Slowly, he begins to realize that from the start he has not been the one who has done the summoning.

The kiss, blurred on the window of a subway car, rockets by them down a tunnel lit by cobalt switches. The tunnel walls are stained with seepage where the train crosses beneath the river. The conductor's voice of rattling static calls out the stops where memories disembark and passion and desire are left behind. The walls of the stations the train rushes by are graffitied with names, dates, and epitaphs. The train hurtles past the station where those who died before their time now stand patiently waiting, and past the station of those who waited too long to die. It passes the station of those who died for love, and the jammed station of those who died for lack of love. A cavalcade of shadows open their eyes an instant and reach out to touch the kiss, to catch it on their extended fingertips—fingertips from which the prints have vanished—but the train is already gone, leaving them behind. Tonight, there's no stopping for loneliness or grief. The third rail, stretched thin, tuned like the string of a violin, senses the ineffable weight of the kiss and seems to shoot forward. Charged with current, the third rail does not belong to the kingdom of the dead, and the kiss follows its path as if tracing a silver thread out of a maze.

A kiss crosses the city. It travels along streets named for coasts—North Shore, Lakeside, Waveland, Surf—that echo as if paved with wet tile. Above the streetlights, nighthawks wheel, yiping like gulls. Beneath windowsills, the shadowy mark of the last tide fades like an impression of elastic on a bare waist.

A kiss crosses the city, floating facedown like a reflection over the dreamers gazing up from a neighborhood of flooded basements and attics. Behind grated shop windows, the mannequins are mermaids; each night they reenter the sea as if drawing a zipper down the spine of a blue-green gown.

Her kiss crosses the city along a bridge arched like the bluest note of a saxophone, an unfinished bridge extending out over a night sea of sweet water. The beacon revolving at its end may be the dome of a squad car or the lantern of a fisherman. Trailing less shadow than a fish, her kiss slips undetected past lamps, past the flashlights of night watchmen, past gates, alarms, curfews. Not even the lips it's meant for feel the secret entry of her tongue, the scrape of her teeth, or, when she pulls away, the clinging thread of briny spit.

# THE RIVER

In the rain, the alley becomes a river that winds through sleepers. Lovers listen to it flow through the dark—or so a man unable to sleep imagines. He can almost hear the river too, although he knows that listening for it may merely be a way of occupying his mind, which should be dreaming. There may be no lovers at all. Even if there are, they may be asleep with mouths opened and backs turned to each other.

It wouldn't be the first time he's measured his life by imagining lovers. He remembers, on a morning when he was younger, standing at the window of the copy room in the high-rise office building in which he worked, and gazing across the busy avenue at the shade-drawn windows of an old hotel that still retained its elegance. Even now, he recalls the surprising rush of emotions when it occurred to him as if he could *sense* it that, while he stood listening to the clatter of Xerox machines, lovers were waking just across the street. Perhaps he'd only imagined the lovers then as well, but at that moment their presence behind the shade-drawn windows seemed so palpable that his own life felt insubstantial beside it, and he was filled with an ache for something he couldn't name but knew was missing. If they were only a daydream, then it was the kind of daydream that sometimes precedes a revelation. That was the morning he'd become certain that he wasn't right for an office job and needed to change the direction of his life while there was still time. A week later, he had quit and returned to school.

Tonight, he senses their presence again. He'd rather

feel the presence of lovers, imaginary though they may be than the absence of the woman he's separated from. If only for a night, they're a respite from the conversation he carries on without her, addressing her as if she can hear him. The lovers are silent. They lie listening to the river, and with his eyes closed he can almost hear it as they must: a high-pitched echo of sewers, a sound of darkness laced with flowing water. Every crack trickles, every overhang drips. Each drop encases its own separate note, the way each drop engulfs its own blue pearl of light.

Between wakefulness and dreaming, with his eyes closed he can see the light reflected by the falling river of rain: fogged streetlamps and taillights streaked along the Outer Drive, a downtown of dimmed office buildings and glowing hotel lobbies, acetylene sparking behind blue factory windows, racks of vigil candles in the cathedral, always kept open, across the street from the neon-lit bus terminal. If he were to rise and walk along the river, he'd see the shades raised and curtains parted, and find himself in a neighborhood where the dark buildings, as he's always suspected, are populated by lovers. Their silhouettes stand undressing, framed in windows, naked and enigmatic like the lovers on a tarot card—men and women, men and men, women and women, embracing. Lovers in the present appear superimposed over lovers from the past so that it's impossible for him to tell who is a shadow of whom. The rooms, parked cars, all the sites of their private histories, glimmer as if their memories have become luminous as spirits. Even the loners are visible beneath single bulbs, appraising their desire in mirrors. The El clatters by above the roofs, its lighted windows like a strip of blue movie.

Nearly asleep, the man listens to the clatter of the El train, fading over viaducts, merging, as it grows distant, with the sounds of sporadic traffic and occasional sirens, all swept along together in the rush of the river. Listening to the river is another way of thinking about the woman. He's drifting on a flood of night thoughts—thoughts he may try to dismiss in daylight, the way dreams are renounced and forgotten, but his restless nights have begun to inform his days. Almost dreaming, with the river flowing beside his ear, he understands why the lovers have been summoned: because the memory of the woman is becoming a shadow, one he carries like a secret, close to his heart; because beside this memory he has grown insubstantial. It draws him along behind it like a shadow—a shadow of a shadow. It has made him dark and incomprehensible even to himself. The lovers from the present have appeared, as they did when he was younger, to remind him that there is only so much time to change the direction of a life. The lovers from the past have appeared because it may already be too late, because it may be time to release his memories so that they can begin to assume a life of their own.

And what about the memory of the boy left at the window, staring out past his own spattered reflection? The boy could disappear behind a single breath fogged on the glass, then wiped away. The room has fallen asleep behind him; the bed, without his weight, is light enough to levitate. Downstairs, the Ukrainian kid, a maestro now, has begun to fiddle a nocturne to pacify the dead. Across the alley, prayers rise like an attar of roses from a basement flat. Love, rain has replaced nighthawks. It drums on the helmet of a blue light. Each drop contains its own blue bulb, and when they shatter they collect into a blue river that continues to gleam. The river, the same river sweeping them both away, is all that connects the boy and the man. It flows through the inland city, down streets it submerges, to the slick highways that bank a black sea of prairie. It empties by the piers where the rusty barges are moored along the ghostly coastline. From his window overlooking the alley that has become a river, the boy can see this. He can see the blue of that single bulb diffused in the sheen of breakwaters and distant winks of pumping stations, in the vague outlines of freighters far out on what, come morning, will be a horizon. He could glimpse the future passing, reflected in the current, if he weren't watching the streetlight slowly sinking as it swirls into the vortex of a sewer, if he weren't still waiting for the silhouettes to come for him. He doesn't realize—he won't ever know—that, like them, he's become a shadow.

# NIGHTHAWKS

The moon, still cooling off from last night, back in the sky—a bulb insects can't circle. Instead, they teem around a corner streetlight, while down the block air conditioners crank, synchronized with katydids.

There's a light on in a garage where a man's legs, looking lonely, stick out from under a Dodge. What is it that's almost tender about someone tinkering with a car after midnight? The askew glare of the extension lamp propped in the open engine reminds me of how once, driving through the dark in Iowa, I saw a man and woman outlined in light, kissing in a wheat field. They stood pressed against each other before the blazing bank of headlamps from a giant combine. It must have been threshing in the dark, for dust and chaff hung smoldering in the beams, making it seem as if the couple stood in smoke or fog.

I was speeding down a gravel-pinging road and caught only a glimpse of them, but took it as an omen to continue following the drunken divorcée I'd met earlier in a roadside bar and grill where I'd stopped for a coffee on my way back to Chicago. *Divorcée* was her word, the way she'd introduced herself. "I'm celebrating becoming an official gay divorcée," she'd told me. I must have looked a little surprised because she quickly added, as if I'd gotten the wrong idea, "You know, not *gay* like with other women, but gay, like, you know, wild." We had several drinks, danced to the jukebox, and ended up in the parking lot, necking in her pickup. When I started to unbutton her blouse, she asked, "You intend to sit out here all night like teenagers or do you want to follow me home?"

I didn't know the countryside. I followed her down highways, one veering into another, so many turns that I thought she must be taking a shortcut. I had the windows rolled down, hoping the streaming night air would clear my head. Beyond the narrow beams of my headlights, I could feel the immensity of prairie buoying us up, stretching in the dark without the limit of a horizon, and I felt suddenly lost in its vastness in a way I'd only felt before on the ocean, rocking at night in a small boat. She kept driving faster, and I could imagine the toe of her high heel pressing down hard on the workboot-size gas pedal of her truck. I wasn't paying attention to where she was leading me and couldn't have kept track if I'd tried. Unlit blacktop tunneled through low hanging trees. By the time we hit the dirt roads she was driving like a maniac, bouncing over railroad crossings and the humps of drainage pipes, dust swirling behind her so that her taillights were only red pinpoints, and I wondered what radio station she must be listening to, wondered if she was drunker than I'd realized and she thought that we were racing, or if she'd had a sudden change of heart and was trying to lose me on those back roads, and I wondered if I ought to let her.

Tonight, a lot of people are still up watching the nighthawks hunt through the streetlights. The white bars on their wings flash, as they dip through the lights, then glide off against the dark trees that line the street. The trees seem more like shadows, except where the inverted cones of light catch their leaves and heighten their green. And despite all the people still awake, unable to let go of the evening, leaning from windows, smoking on steps or rocking on front porches, it's quiet—no small talk, or gossip, no stories, or lullabies—only the whir of insects and the stabbing cries of birds, as if we all know we should be sleeping now, leaving the night-hawks to describe the night.

# THE WOMAN
# WHO FAINTED

During Sunday mass in summer, a woman sometimes fainted. She fainted at the 11:15 mass which, during summer, was the last mass of the day. By then, banded shafts of sunlight streamed through the towering stained glass windows, and not even the cool marble and plaster of the church could keep out the heat. Despite the heat, the men in the Holy Name Society who served as ushers wore suits and ties. Their Holy Name pins glinted from their lapels as they escorted parishioners down the aisles to empty spaces in the pews. The 11:15 mass was always crowded. I thought of it as the adult mass. When I'd been a student at St. Roman's Grade School, we were expected to attend mass at 9:00 a.m. and to sit with our classes under the vigilant eyes of nuns. There weren't any nuns to be seen at the 11:15 mass. Women dressed for it as if they were going out for the evening. I would find a seat in the choir loft from which I could look over the rows of crowded pews for the woman who fainted.

Even in the crowded church I could find her. She always wore her hair pinned up, ballerina style, exposing her slender neck, and the same summer dress, a blue-green that I imagined she'd matched to the shade of her eyes. It was sleeveless, revealing the curve of her shoulders; the seam of the zipper down the back traced the contour of her slim waist and hips. Surrounded by women in flowered prints and polka dots, she was easy to spot. Everything about her seemed graceful: the way she made the sign of the cross, then folded her hands to pray, the willowy motion of her body as she knelt and stood and sat in response to the mass. I'd never seen her anywhere but at church. She made going to mass bearable. I would have watched her whether she fainted or not.

That summer, after my sophomore year in high school, was the last summer I went to church. I went only because I didn't want my family to feel that, yet again, they'd failed to pass on something they believed was essential. They had sent me to Catholic grade school, where every morning began with a mass—usually a requiem mass or a mass for the feast day of a martyr. Perhaps I had already attended too many masses. I was bored and had come to resent the suffering, death, and, even more, the fear underlying religion. To be free of the fear, it seemed necessary to be free of the faith. I knelt daydreaming about the woman while the mass blurred around me. I imagined her after mass, alone in an empty room, drawing the blinds and then drawing the zipper down the length of the blue-green dress. I could remember a time not long before when I believed such thoughts, especially during mass, were a sin for which I could burn. Now, the only sin that worried me was that she might somehow sense the weight of my stare on the back of her bare neck. It would be wrong to intrude on her in any way. In the crowded church, she seemed to kneel alone at the private center of her own devotion. Watching her, I thought that if I could pray with such fervor I would still believe in those saints and angels of my childhood who gazed down from the domed ceiling of the old Polish church.

Then, sometimes, before my eyes she would begin to faint. I recognized immediately the small adjustments fainting brought on: her hand sweeping across her forehead as if brushing back hair held perfectly in place; the crescent of sweat staining her dress. By the Sanctus she wavered as she stood. I could almost feel the heat as I imagined she felt it: each candle flame flickering another unnecessary degree against her flushed cheeks, the steaminess of the perspiring bodies around her, the hot exhalations of all that chanting and singing. It amazed me that no one else paid any attention to her. All around the church, women knelt fanning with hymn books. Her hymn book dropped from her hand to the pew before her. A single fan whirred over the pulpit as if preaching a sermon. The Cupidlike cherubim and graver seraphim gazed down impassively from the firmament of the nave. Perhaps she was praying fervently, *Please, Lord, don't let me faint again.* If so, it was a prayer that went unanswered.

Her head droops; she tries to prop herself up with her elbows, but slumps clutching the top of the pew with one hand as she sinks between the bench and kneeler. Finally, the woman next to her has noticed and awkwardly tries to help her to the seat, but it's too late, she is sliding down, drifting, collapsing to the marble floor with a thump that draws heads from all over the church and brings the Holy Name ushers rushing from their stations. They gather her in their arms and hurriedly carry her—throat flushed and mottled, eyes rolling open and closed, sweaty tendrils of hair undone, lips moaning as if continuing to pray—along the center aisle of the packed church, pausing only a moment as the hand of an old woman in a babushka darts out from a pew to tug down the hem of the blue-green dress that has ridden up those slender thighs.

# HOT ICE

## SAINTS

The saint, a virgin, was uncorrupted. She had been frozen in a block of ice many years ago.

Her father had found her half-naked body floating facedown among water lilies, her blond hair fanning at the marshy edge of the overgrown duck pond people still referred to as the Douglas Park Lagoon.

That's how Eddie Kapusta had heard it.

Douglas Park was a black park now, the lagoon curdled in milky green scum as if it had soured, and Kapusta didn't doubt that were he to go there they'd find his body floating in the lily pads too. But sometimes in winter, riding by on the California Avenue bus, the park flocked white, deserted, and the lagoon frozen over, Eddie could almost picture what it had been back then: swans gliding around the small, wooded island at the center, and rowboats plying into sunlight from the gaping stone tunnels of the haunted-looking boathouse.

The girl had gone rowing with a couple of guys—

some said they were sailors, neighborhood kids going off to the war—nobody ever said who exactly or why she went with them, as if it didn't matter. They rowed her around to the blind side of the little island. Nobody knew what happened there either. It was necessary for each person to imagine it for himself.

They were only joking at first was how Kapusta imagined it, laughing at her broken English, telling her to be friendly or swim home. One of them stroked her hair, gently undid her bun, and as her hair fell cascading over her shoulders surprising them all, the other reached too suddenly for the buttons on her blouse; she tore away so hard the boat rocked violently, her slip and bra split, breasts sprung loose, she dove.

Even the suddenness was slow motion the way Kapusta imagined it. But once they were in the water the rest went through his mind in a flash—the boat capsizing, the sailors thrashing for the little island, and the girl struggling alone in that sepia water too warm from summer, just barely deep enough for bullheads, with a mud bottom kids said was quicksand exploding into darkness with each kick. He didn't want to wonder what she remembered as she held her last breath underwater. His mind raced over that to her father wading out into cattails, scooping her half-naked and still limp from the resisting water lilies, and running with her in his arms across the park crying in Polish or Slovak or Bohemian, whatever they were, and then riding with her on the streetcar he wouldn't let stop until it reached the icehouse he owned, where crazy with grief he sealed her in ice.

"I believe it up to the part about the streetcar," Manny Santora said that summer when they told each other such stories, talking often about things Manny called *weirdness* while pitching quarters in front of Buddy's Bar. "I don't believe he hijacked no streetcar, man."

"What you think, man, he called a cab?" Pancho, Manny's older brother, asked, winking at Eddie as if he'd scored.

Every time they talked like this Manny and Pancho argued. Pancho believed in everything—ghosts, astrology, legends. His nickname was Padrecito, which went back to his days as an altar boy when he would dress up as a priest and hold mass in the backyard with hosts punched with bottle caps from stale tortillas and real wine he'd collected from bottles the winos had left on door stoops. Eddie's nickname was Eduardo, though the only person who called him that was Manny, who had made it up. Manny wasn't the kind of guy to have a nickname—he was Manny or Santora.

Pancho believed if you played certain rock songs backward you'd hear secret messages from the devil. He believed in devils and angels. He still believed he had a guardian angel. It was something like being lucky, like making the sign of the cross before you stepped into the batter's box. "It's why I don't get caught even when I'm caught," he'd say when the cops would catch him dealing and not take him in. Pancho believed in saints. For a while he had even belonged to a gang called the Saints. They'd tried to recruit Manny too, who, though younger, was tougher than Pancho, but Manny had no use for gangs. "I already belong to the Loners," he said.

Pancho believed in the girl in ice. In sixth grade, Sister Joachim, the ancient nun in charge of the altar boys, had told him the girl should be canonized and that she'd secretly written to the pope informing him that already there had been miracles and cures. "All the martyrs didn't die in Rome," she'd told Pancho. "They're still suffering today in China and Russia and Korea and even here in your own neighborhood." Like all nuns she loved Pancho. Dressed in his surplice and cassock he looked as if he should be beatified himself, a young St. Sebastian or Juan de la Cruz, the only altar boy in the history of the parish to spend his money on different-colored gym shoes so they would match the priest's vestments—red for martyrs, white for feast days, black for requiems. The nuns knew he punished himself during Lent, offering up his pain for the poor souls in purgatory.

Their love for Pancho had made things impossible for Manny in the Catholic school. He seemed Pancho's opposite in almost every way and dropped out after they'd held him back in sixth grade. He switched to public school, but mostly he hung out on the streets.

"I believe she worked miracles right in this neighborhood, man," Pancho said.

"Bullshit, man. Like what miracles?" Manny wanted to know.

"Okay, man, you know Big Antek," Pancho said.

"Big Antek the wino?"

They all knew Big Antek. He bought them beer. He'd been a butcher in every meat market in the neighborhood, but drunkenly kept hacking off pieces of his hands, and finally quit completely to become a full-time alky.

Big Antek had told Pancho about working on Kedzie Avenue when it was still mostly people from the old country and he had found a job at a Czech meat market with sawdust on the floor and skinned rabbits in the window. He wasn't there a week when he got so drunk he passed out in the freezer and when he woke the door was locked and everyone was gone. It was Saturday and he knew they wouldn't open again until Monday and by then he'd be stiff as a two-by-four. He was already shivering so badly he couldn't stand still or he'd fall over. He figured he'd be dead already except that his blood was half alcohol. Parts of him were going numb and he started staggering around, bumping past hanging sides of meat, singing, praying out loud, trying to let the fear out before it became panic. He knew it was hopeless, but he was looking anyway for some place to smash out, some plug to pull, something to stop the cold. At the back of the freezer, behind racks of meat, he found a cooler. It was an old one, the kind that used to stand packed with blocks of ice and bottles of beer in taverns during the war. And seeing it, Big Antek suddenly remembered a moment from his first summer back from the Pacific, discharged from the hospital in Manila and back in Buddy's lounge on Twenty-fourth Street, kitty-corner from a victory garden where a plaque erroneously listed his name among the parish war dead. It was an ordinary moment, nothing dramatic like his life flashing before his eyes, but the memory filled him with such clarity that the freezer became dreamlike beside it. The ball game was on the radio over at Buddy's, DiMaggio in center again, while Bing Crosby crooned from the jukebox, which was playing at the same time. Antek was reaching into Buddy's cooler, up to his elbow in ice water feeling for a beer, while looking out through the open tavern door that framed Twenty-fourth Street as if it were a movie full of girls blurred in brightness, slightly over-exposed blondes, a movie he could step into any time he chose now that he was home; but right at this moment he was taking his time, stretching it out until it encompassed his entire life, the cold bottles bobbing away from his fingertips, clunking against the ice, until finally he grabbed one, hauled it up dripping, wondering what he'd grabbed—a Monarch or Yusay Pilsner or Fox Head 400—then popped the cork in the opener on the side of the cooler, the foam rising as he tilted his head back and let it pour down his throat, privately celebrating being alive. That moment was what drinking had once been about. It was a good thing to be remembering now when he was dying with nothing else to do about it. He had the funny idea of climbing inside the cooler and going to sleep to continue the memory like a dream. The cooler was thick with frost, so white it seemed to glow. Its lid had been replaced with a slab of dry ice that smoked even within the cold of the freezer, reminding Antek that as kids they'd always called it hot ice. He nudged it aside. Beneath it was a block of ice as clear as if the icemen had just delivered it. There was something frozen inside. He glanced away but knew already, immediately, it was a body. He couldn't move away. He looked again. The longer he stared, the calmer he felt. It was a girl. He could make out her hair, not just blonde but radiating gold like a candle flame behind a window in winter. Her breasts were bare. The ice seemed even clearer. She was beautiful and dreamy looking, not dreamy like sleeping, but the dreamy look DPs sometimes get when they first come to the city. As long as he stayed beside her he didn't shiver. He could feel the blood return; he was warm as if

the smoldering dry ice really was hot. He spent the
weekend huddled against her, and early Monday morning when the Czech opened the freezer he said to Antek,
"Get out . . . you're fired." That's all either one of them
said.

"You know what I think," Pancho said. "They moved
her body from the icehouse to the butcher shop because
the cops checked, man."

"You know what I think," Manny said, "I think
you're doing so much shit that even the winos can
bullshit you."

They looked hard at one another, Manny especially
looking bad because of a beard he was trying to grow
that was mostly stubble except for a black knot of hair
frizzing from the cleft under his lower lip—a little lip
beard like a jazz musician's—and Pancho covered in
crosses, a wooden one dangling from a leather thong
over his open shirt, and small gold cross on a fine gold
chain tight about his throat, and a tiny platinum cross in
his right earlobe, and a faded India-ink cross tattooed on
his wrist where one would feel for a pulse.

"He got a cross-shaped dick," Manny said.

"Only when I got a hard-on, man," Pancho said,
grinning, and they busted up.

"Hey, Eddie, man," Pancho said, "what you think of
all this, man?"

Kapusta just shrugged as he always did. Not that he
didn't have any ideas exactly, or that he didn't care. That
shrug *was* what Kapusta believed.

"Yeah. Well, man," Pancho said, "I believe there's
saints, and miracles happening everywhere only everybody's afraid to admit it. I mean like Ralph's little brother,

the blue baby who died when he was eight. He knew he was dying all his life, man, and never complained. He was a saint. Or Big Antek who everybody says is a wino, man. But he treats everybody as human beings. Who you think's more of a saint—him or the president, man? And Mrs. Corillo who everybody thought was crazy because she was praying loud all the time. Remember? She kneeled all day praying for Puerto Rico during that earthquake—the one Roberto Clemente crashed on the way to, going to help. Remember that, man? Mrs. Corillo prayed all day and they thought she was still praying at night and she was kneeling there dead. She was a saint, man, and so's Roberto Clemente. There should be like a church, St. Roberto Clemente. With a statue of him in his batting stance by the altar. Kids could pray to him at night. That would mean something to them."

"The earthquake wasn't in Puerto Rico, man," Manny told him, "and I don't believe no streetcar'd stop for somebody carrying a dead person."

## AMNESIA

It was hard to believe there ever were streetcars. The city back then, the city of their fathers, which was as far back as a family memory extended, even the city of their childhoods, seemed as remote to Eddie and Manny as the capital of some foreign country.

The past collapsed about them—decayed, bulldozed, obliterated. They walked past block-length gutted factories, past walls of peeling, multicolored doors hammered up around flooded excavation pits, hung out in half-boarded storefronts of groceries that had shut down when they were kids, dusty cans still stacked on the shelves. Broken glass collected everywhere, mounding like sand in the little, sunken front yards and gutters. Even the church's stained-glass windows were patched with plywood.

They could vaguely remember something different before the cranes and wrecking balls gradually moved in, not order exactly, but rhythms: five-o'clock whistles, air-raid sirens on Tuesdays, Thursdays when the stockyards blew over like a brown wind of boiling hooves and bone, at least that's what people said, screwing up their faces: "Phew! They're making glue today!"

Streetcar tracks were long paved over; black webs of trolley wires vanished. So did the victory gardens that had become weed beds taking the corroded plaques with the names of neighborhood dead with them.

Things were gone they couldn't remember but missed; and things were gone they weren't sure ever were there— the pickle factory by the railroad tracks where a DP with a net worked scooping rats out of the open vats, troughs for ragmen's horses, ragmen and their wooden wagons, knife sharpeners pushing screeching whetstones up alleys hollering "Scissors! Knives!," hermits living in cardboard shacks behind billboards.

At times, walking past the gaps, they felt as if they were no longer quite there themselves, half-lost despite familiar street signs, shadows of themselves superimposed on the present, except there was no present— everything either rubbled past or promised future—and they were walking as if floating, getting nowhere as if they'd smoked too much grass.

That's how it felt those windy nights that fall when Manny and Eddie circled the county jail. They'd float down California past the courthouse, Bridwell Correctional, the auto pound, Communicable Disease Hospital, and then follow the long, curving concrete wall of the prison back toward Twenty-sixth Street, sharing a joint, passing it with cupped hands, ready to flip it if a cop should cruise by, but one place you could count on not to see cops was outside the prison.

Nobody was there; just the wall, railroad tracks, the river, and the factories that lined it—boundaries that remained intact while neighborhoods came and went.

Eddie had never noticed any trees, but swirls of leaves scuffed past their shoes. It was Kapusta's favorite weather, wild, blowing nights that made him feel free, flagpoles knocking in the wind, his clothes flapping like flags. He felt both tight and loose, and totally alive even walking down a street that always made him sad. It was the street that followed the curve of the prison wall, and it didn't have a name. It was hardly a street at all, more a shadow of the wall, potholed, puddled, half-paved, rutted with rusted railroad tracks.

"Trains used to go down this street." Manny said.

"I seen tanks going down this street."

"Tank cars?"

"No, army tanks," Kapusta said.

"Battleships too, Eduardo?" Manny asked seriously. Then the wind ripped a laugh from his mouth that was loud enough to carry over the prison wall.

Kapusta laughed loud too. But he *could* remember tanks, camouflaged with netting, rumbling on flatcars, their cannons outlined by the red lanterns of the dinging crossing gates that were down all along Twenty-sixth Street. It was one of the first things he remembered. He must have been very small. The train seemed endless. He could see the guards in the turrets on the prison wall watching it, the only time he'd ever seen them facing the street. "Still sending them to Korea or someplace," his father had said, and for years after Eddie believed you could get to Korea by train. For years after, he would wake in the middle of the night when it was quiet enough to hear the trains passing blocks away, and lie in bed listening, wondering if the tanks were rumbling past the prison, if not to Korea then to some other war that tanks went to at night; and he would think of the prisoners in their cells locked up for their violence with knives and clubs and cleavers and pistols, and wonder if they were lying awake, listening too as the netted cannons rolled by their barred windows. Even as a child Eddie knew the names of men inside there: Milo Hermanski, who had stabbed some guy in the eye in a fight at Andy's Tap; Billy Gomez, who set the housing project on fire every time his sister Gina got gangbanged; Ziggy's uncle, the war hero, who one day blew off the side of Ziggy's mother's face while she stood ironing her slip during an argument over a will; and other names of people he didn't know but had heard about—Benny Bedwell, with his "Elvis" sideburns, who may have killed the Grimes sister; Mafia hit men; bank robbers; junkies; perverts; murderers on death row—he could sense them lying awake listening, could feel the tension of their sleeplessness, and Pancho lay among them now as Eddie and Manny walked outside the wall.

They stopped again as they'd been stopping and

yelled together: "Pancho, Panchooooooo," dragging out the last vowel the way they had as kids standing on the sidewalk calling up at one another's windows, as if knocking at the door were not allowed.

"Pancho, we're out here, brother, me and Eddie," Manny shouted. "Hang tough, man, we ain't forgetting you."

Nobody answered. They kept walking, stopping to shout at intervals the way they had been doing almost every night.

"If only we knew what building he was in," Eddie said.

They could see the upper stories of the brick buildings rising over the wall, their grated windows low lit, never dark, floodlights on the roof glaring down.

"Looks like a factory, man," Eddie said. "Looks like the same guy who planned the Harvester foundry on Western did the jail."

"You rather be in the army or in there?" Manny asked.

"No way they're getting me in there," Eddie said.

That was when Eddie knew Pancho was crazy, when the judge had given Pancho a choice at the end of his trial.

"You're a nice-looking kid," the judge had said, "too nice for prison. What do you want to do with your life?"

"Pose for holy cards," Pancho said, "St. Joseph is my specialty." Pancho was standing there wearing the tie they had brought him wound around his head like an Indian headband. He was wearing a black satin jacket with the signs of the zodiac on the back.

"I'm going to give you a chance to straighten out, to gain some self-respect. The court's attitude would be very sympathetic to any signs of self-direction and patriotism, joining the army, for instance."

"I'm a captain," Pancho told him.

"The army or jail, which is it?"

"I'm a captain, man, *soy capitán, capitán,*" Pancho insisted, humming "La Bamba" under his breath.

"You're a misfit."

Manny was able to visit Pancho every three weeks. Each time it got worse. Sometimes Pancho seemed hardly to recognize him, looking away, refusing to meet Manny's eyes the whole visit. Sometimes he'd cry. For a while at first he wanted to know how things were in the neighborhood. Then he stopped asking, and when Manny tried to tell him the news Pancho would get jumpy, irritable, and lapse into total silence. "I don't wanna talk about out there, man," he told Manny. "I don't wanna remember that world until I'm ready to step into it again. You remember too much in here you go crazy, man. I wanna forget everything, like I never existed."

"His fingernails are gone, man," Manny told Eddie. "He's gnawing on himself like a rat, and when I ask him what's going down all he'll say is 'I'm locked in hell, my angel's gone, I've lost my luck'—bullshit like that, you know? Last time I seen him he says, 'I'm gonna kill myself, man, if they don't stop hitting on me.'"

"I can't fucking believe it. I can't fucking believe he's in there," Eddie said. "He should be in a monastery somewhere; he should've been a priest. He had a vocation."

"He had a vocation to be an altar boy, man," Manny said, spitting it out as if he was disgusted by what he was saying, talking down about his own brother. "It was that nuns-and-priests crap that messed up his head. He was happy being an altar boy, man, if they'd've let him be an altar boy all his life he'd still be happy."

By the time they were halfway down the nameless street it was drizzling a fine, misty spray, and Manny was yelling in Spanish, *"Estamos contigo, hermano! San Roberto Clemente te ayudará!"*

They broke into "La Bamba," Eddie singing in Spanish too, not sure exactly what he was singing, but it sounded good: *"Yo no soy marinero, soy capitán, capitán, ay, ay Bamba! ay, ay, Bamba!"* He had lived beside Spanish in the neighborhood all his life, and every so often a word got through, like *juilota*, which was what Manny called pigeons when they used to hunt them with slingshots under the railroad bridges. It seemed a perfect word to Eddie, one in which he could hear both their cooing and the whistling rush of their wings. He didn't remember any words like that in Polish, which his grandma had spoken to him when he was little, and which, Eddie had been told, he could once speak too.

By midnight they were at the end of their circuit, emerging from the unlighted, nameless street, stepping over tracks that continued to curve past blinded switches. Under the streetlights on Twenty-sixth the prison wall appeared rust stained, oozing at the cracks. The wire spooled at the top of the wall looked rusty in the wet light, as did the tracks as if the rain were rusting everything overnight.

They stopped on the corner of Twenty-sixth where the old icehouse stood across the nameless street from the prison. One could still buy ice from a vending machine in front. Without realizing it, Eddie guarded his breathing as if still able to detect the faintest stab of ammonia, although it had been a dozen years since the louvered fans on the icehouse roof had clacked through clouds of vapor.

"Padrecitooooo!" they both hollered.

Their voices bounced back off the wall.

They stood on the corner by the icehouse as if waiting around for someone. From there they could stare down Twenty-sixth—five dark blocks, then an explosion of neon at Kedzie Avenue: taco places, bars, a street plugged in, winking festive as a pinball machine, traffic from it coming toward them in the rain.

The streetlights surged and flickered.

"You see that?" Eddie asked. "They used to say when the streetlights flickered it meant they just fried somebody in the electric chair."

"So much bullshit," Manny said. *"Compadre, no te rajes!"* he yelled at the wall.

"Whatcha tell him?"

"It sounds different in English," Manny said. " 'Godfather, do not give up.' It's words from an old song."

Kapusta stepped out into the middle of Twenty-sixth and stood in the misting drizzle squinting at Kedzie through cupped hands, as if he held binoculars. He could make out the traffic light way down there changing to green. He could almost hear the music from the bars that would serve them without asking for IDs so long as Manny was there. "You thirsty by any chance, man?" he asked.

"You buyin' by any chance, man?" Manny said, grinning.

*"Buenas noches,* Pancho," they hollered. "Catch you tomorrow, man."

"Good night, guys," a falsetto voice echoed back from over the wall.

"That ain't Pancho," Manny said.

"Sounds like the singer on old Platters' records," Eddie said. "Ask him if he knows Pancho, man."

"Hey, you know a guy named Pancho Santora?" Manny called.

"Oh, Pancho?" the voice inquired.

"Yeah, Pancho."

"Oh, Cisco!" the voice shouted. They could hear him cackling. "Hey, baby, I don't know no Pancho. Is that rain I smell?"

"It's raining," Eddie hollered.

"Hey, baby, tell me something. What's it like out there tonight?"

Manny and Eddie looked at each other. "Beautiful!" they yelled together.

## GRIEF

There was never a requiem, but by Lent everyone knew that one way or another Pancho was gone. No wreaths, but plenty of rumors: Pancho had hung himself in his cell; his throat had been slashed in the showers; he'd killed another inmate and was under heavy sedation in a psycho ward at Kankakee. And there was talk he'd made a deal and was in the army, shipped off to a war he had sworn he'd never fight; that he had turned snitch and had been secretly relocated with a new identity; or that he had become a trustee and had simply walked away while mowing the grass in front of the courthouse, escaped maybe to Mexico, or maybe just across town to the North Side around Diversey where, if one made the rounds of the leather bars, they might see someone with

Pancho's altar-boy eyes staring out from the makeup of a girl.

Some saw him late at night like a ghost haunting the neighborhood, collar up, in the back of the church lighting a vigil candle; or veiled in a black mantilla, speeding past, face floating by on a greasy El window.

Rumors were becoming legends, but there was never a wake, never an obituary, and no one knew how to mourn a person who had just disappeared.

For a while Manny disappeared too. He wasn't talking, and Kapusta didn't ask. They had quit walking around the prison wall months before, around Christmas when Pancho refused to let anyone, even Manny, visit. But their night walks had been tapering off before that.

Eddie remembered the very last time they had walked beside the wall together. It was in December, and he was frozen from standing around a burning garbage can on Kedzie, selling Christmas trees. About ten, when the lot closed, Manny came by and they stopped to thaw out at the Carta Blanca. A guy named José kept buying them whiskeys, and they staggered out after midnight into a blizzard.

"Look at this white bullshit," Manny said.

Walking down Twenty-sixth they stopped to fling snowballs over the wall. Then they decided to stand there singing Christmas carols. Snow was drifting against the wall, erasing the street that had hardly been there. Eddie could tell Manny was starting to go silent. Manny would get the first few words into a carol, singing at the top of his voice, then stop as if choked by the song. His eyes stayed angry when he laughed. Everything was bullshit to him, and finally Eddie couldn't talk to him anymore. Stomping away from the prison through fresh snow, Eddie had said, "If this keeps up, man, I'll need boots."

"It don't *have* to *keep up*, man," Manny snapped. "Nobody's making you come, man. It ain't your brother."

"All I said is I'll need boots, man," Eddie said.

"You said it hopeless, man; things are always fucking hopeless to you."

"Hey, you're the big realist, man," Eddie told him.

"I never said I was no realist," Manny mumbled.

Kapusta hadn't had a lot of time since then. He had dropped out of school again and was loading trucks at night for UPS. One more semester didn't matter, he figured, and he needed some new clothes, cowboy boots, a green leather jacket. The weather had turned drizzly and mild—a late Easter but an early spring. Eddie had heard Manny was hanging around by himself, still finding bullshit everywhere, only worse. Now he muttered as he walked like some crazy, bitter old man, or one of those black guys reciting the gospel to buildings, telling off posters and billboards, neon signs, stoplights, passing traffic—bullshit, all of it bullshit.

It was Tuesday in Holy Week, the statues inside the church shrouded in violet, when Eddie slipped on his green leather jacket and walked over to Manny's before going to work. He rang the doorbell, then stepped outside in the rain and stood on the sidewalk under Manny's windows, watching cars pass.

After a while Manny came down the stairs and slammed out the door.

"How you doin', man?" Eddie said as if they'd just run into each other by accident.

Manny stared at him. "How far'd you have to chase him for that jacket, man?" he said.

"I knew you'd dig it." Eddie smiled.

They went out for a few beers later that night, after midnight, when Eddie was through working, but instead of going to a bar they ended up just walking. Manny had rolled a couple bombers and they walked down the boulevard along California watching the headlights flash by like a procession of candles. Manny still wasn't saying much, but they were passing the reefer like having a conversation. At Thirty-first, by the Communicable Disease Hospital, Eddie figured they would follow the curve of the boulevard toward the bridge on Western, but Manny turned as if out of habit toward the prison.

They were back walking along the wall. There was still old ice from winter at the base of it.

"The only street in Chicago where it's still winter," Eddie mumbled.

"Remember yelling?" Manny said, almost in a whisper.

"Sure," Eddie nodded.

"Called, joked, prayed, sang Christmas songs, remember that night, how cold we were, man?"

"Yeah."

"What a bunch of stupid bullshit, huh?"

Eddie was afraid Manny was going to start the bullshit stuff again. Manny had stopped and stood looking at the wall.

Then he cupped his hands over his mouth and yelled, "Hey! You dumb fuckers in there! We're back! Can you hear me? Hey, wake up, niggers, hey, spics, hey, honkies, you buncha fuckin' monkeys in cages, hey! We're out here *free!*"

"Hey, Manny, come on, man," Eddie said.

Manny uncupped his hands, shook his head, and smiled. They took a few steps, then Manny whirled back again. "We're out here free, man! We're smokin' reefer, drinking cold beer while you're in there, you assholes! We're on our way to fuck your wives, man, your girlfriends are giving us blow jobs while you jack-offs flog it. Hey, man, I'm pumping your old lady out here right now. She likes it in the ass like you!"

"What are you doing, man?" Eddie was pleading. "Take it easy."

Manny was screaming his lungs out, almost incoherent, shouting every filthy thing he could think of, and voices, the voices they'd never heard before, had begun shouting back from the other side of the wall.

"Shadup! Shadup! Shadup out there, you crazy fuck!" came the voices.

"She's out here licking my balls while you're punking each other through the bars of your cage!"

"Shadup!" they were yelling, and then a voice howling over the others: "I'll kill you, motherfucker! When I get out you're dead!"

"Come on out," Manny was yelling. "Come and get me, you pieces of shit, you sleazeballs, you scumbag cocksuckers, you creeps are missing it all, your lives are wasted garbage!"

Now there were too many voices to distinguish, whole tiers, whole buildings yelling and cursing and threatening, *shadup, shadup, shadup*, almost a chant, and then the searchlight from the guardhouse slowly turned and swept the street.

"We gotta get outa here," Eddie said, pulling Manny

away. He dragged him to the wall, right up against it where the light couldn't follow, and they started to run, stumbling along the banked strip of filthy ice, dodging stunted trees that grew out at odd angles, running toward Twenty-sixth until Eddie heard the sirens.

"This way, man," he panted, yanking Manny back across the nameless street, jumping puddles and tracks, cutting down a narrow corridor between abandoned truck docks seconds before a squad car, blue dome light revolving, sped past.

They jogged behind the truck docks, not stopping until they came up behind the icehouse. Manny's panting sounded almost like laughing, the way people laugh after they've hurt themselves.

"I hate those motherfuckers," Manny gasped, "all of them, the fucking cops and guards and fucking wall and the bastards behind it. All of them. That must be what makes me a realist, huh, Eddie? I fucking hate them all."

They went back the next night.

Sometimes a thing wasn't a sin—if there was such a thing as sin—Eddie thought, until it's done a second time. There were accidents, mistakes that could be forgiven once; it was repeating them that made them terribly wrong. That was how Eddie felt about going back the next night.

Manny said he was going whether Eddie came or not, so Eddie went, afraid to leave Manny on his own, even though he'd already had trouble trying to get some sleep before going to work. Eddie could still hear the voices yelling from behind the wall and dreamed they were all being electrocuted, electrocuted slowly, by degrees of their crimes, screaming with each surge of current and flicker of streetlights as if in a hell where electricity had replaced fire.

Standing on the dark street Wednesday night, outside the wall again, felt like an extension of his nightmare: Manny raging almost out of control, shouting curses and insults, baiting them over the wall the way a child tortures penned watchdogs, until he had what seemed like the entire west side of the prison howling back, the guards sweeping the street with searchlights, sirens wailing toward them from both Thirty-first and Twenty-sixth.

This time they raced down the tracks that curved toward the river, picking their way in the dark along the junkyard bank, flipping rusted cables of moored barges, running through the fire truck graveyard, following the tracks across the blackened trestles where they'd once shot pigeons and from which they could gaze across the industrial prairie that stretched behind factories all the way to the skyline of downtown. The skyscrapers glowed like luminescent peaks in the misty spring night. Manny and Eddie stopped in the middle of the trestle and leaned over the railing catching their breath.

"Downtown ain't as far away as I used to think when I was a kid." Manny panted.

"These tracks'll take you right there," Eddie said quietly, "to railroad yards under the street, right by the lake."

"How you know, man?"

"A bunch of us used to hitch rides on the boxcars in seventh grade." Eddie was talking very quietly, looking away.

"I usually take the bus, you know?" Manny tried joking.

"I ain't goin' back there with you tomorrow," Eddie said. "I ain't goin' back with you ever."

Manny kept staring off toward the lights downtown as if he hadn't heard. "Okay," he finally said, more to himself, as if surrendering. "Okay, how about tomorrow we do something else, man?"

## NOSTALGIA

They didn't go back.

The next night, Thursday, Eddie overslept and called in sick for work. He tried to get back to sleep but kept falling into half-dreams in which he could hear the voices shouting behind the prison wall. Finally he got up and opened a window. It was dark out. A day had passed almost unnoticed, and now the night felt as if it were a part of the night before, and the night before a part of the night before that, all connected by his restless dreams, fragments of the same continuous night.

Eddie had said that at some point: "It's like one long night," and later Manny had said the same thing as if it had suddenly occurred to him.

They were strung out almost from the start, drifting stoned under the El tracks before Eddie even realized they weren't still sitting on the stairs in front of Manny's house. That was where Eddie had found him, watching traffic, taking sips out of a bottle of Gallo into which Manny had dropped several hits of speed.

Cars gunned by with their windows rolled down and radios playing loud. It sounded like a summer night.

"Ain't you hot wearin' that jacket, man?" Manny asked him.

"Now that you mention it," Eddie said. He was sweating.

Eddie took his leather jacket off and they knotted a handkerchief around one of the cuffs, then slipped the Gallo bottle down the sleeve. They walked along under the El tracks passing a joint. A train, only two cars long, rattled overhead.

"So what we doing, Eduardo?" Manny kept repeating.

"Walking," Eddie said.

"I feel like doing *something*, you know?"

"We are doing something," Eddie insisted.

Eddie led them over to the Coconut Club on Twenty-second. They couldn't get in, but Eddie wanted to look at the window with its neon-green palm tree and winking blue coconuts.

"That's maybe my favorite window," he said.

"You drag me all the way here to see your favorite window, man?!" Manny said.

"It's those blue coconuts," Eddie tried explaining. His mouth was dry, but he couldn't stop talking. He started telling Manny how he had collected windows from the time he was a little kid, even though talking about it made it sound as if windows were more important to him than they actually were. Half the time he was only vaguely aware of collecting them. He would see a window from a bus, like the Greek butcher shop on Halsted with its pyramid of lamb skulls, and make a mental photograph of it. He had special windows all over the city. It was how he held the city together in his mind.

"I'd see all these windows from the El," Eddie said, "when I'd visit my *busha*, my grandma. Like I remember we'd pass this one building where the curtains were all slips hanging by their straps—black ones, white ones, red ones. At night you could see the light bulbs shining through the lace tops. My *busha* said Gypsies lived there." Eddie was walking down the middle of the street, jacket flung over his shoulder, staring up at the windows as if looking for the Gypsies as he talked.

"Someday they're gonna get you as a peeper, man." Manny laughed. "And when they do, don't try explaining to them about this thing of yours for windows, Eduardo."

They were walking down Spaulding back toward Twenty-sixth. The streetlights beamed brighter and brighter, and Manny put his sunglasses on. A breeze was blowing that felt warmer than the air, and they took their shirts off. They saw rats darting along the curb into the sewer on the other side of the street and put their shirts back on.

"The rats get crazy where they start wrecking these old buildings," Manny said.

The cranes and wrecking balls and urban-renewal signs were back with the early spring. They walked around a barricaded site. Water trickled along the gutters from an open hydrant, washing brick dust and debris toward the sewers.

"Can you smell that, man?" Manny asked him, suddenly excited. "I can smell the lake through the hydrant."

"Smells like rust to me," Eddie said.

"I can smell fish! Smelt—the smelt are in! I can smell them right through the hydrant!"

"Smelt?" Eddie said.

"You ain't ever had smelt?" Manny asked. "Little silver fish!"

They caught the Twenty-sixth Street bus—the Polish Zephyr, people called it—going east toward the lake. The back of the bus was empty. They sat in the swaying, long backseat, taking hits out of the bottle in Eddie's sleeve.

"It's usually too early for them yet, but they're out there, Eduardo," Manny kept reassuring him, as if they were actually going fishing.

Eddie nodded. He didn't know anything about smelt. The only fish he ate was canned tuna, but it felt good to be riding somewhere with the windows open and Manny acting more like his old self—sure of himself, laughing easily. Eddie still felt like talking, but his molars were grinding on speed.

The bus jolted down the dark block past Kedzie and was flying when it passed the narrow street between the ice house and the prison, but Eddie and Manny caught a glimpse out the back window of the railroad tracks that curved down the nameless street. The tracks were lined with fuming red flares that threw a red reflection off the concrete walls. Eddie was sure the flares had been set there for them.

Eddie closed his eyes and sank into the rocking of the bus. Even with his eyes closed he could see the reddish glare of the walls. The glare was ineradicable, at the back of his sockets. The wall had looked the same way it had looked in his dreams. They rode in silence.

"It's like one long night," Eddie said somewhere along the way.

His jaws were really grinding and his legs had forgotten gravity by the time they got to the lakefront. They didn't know the time, but it must have been around 3:00 or 4:00 a.m. and the smelt fishers were still out. The lights of their kerosene lanterns reflected along the break-water over the glossy black lake. Eddie and Manny could hear the water lapping under the pier and the fishermen talking in low voices in different languages.

"My uncle Carlos would talk to the fish," Manny said. "No shit. He'd talk to them in Spanish. He didn't have no choice. Whole time here he couldn't speak English. Said it made his brain stuck. We used to come fishing here all the time—smelt, perch, everything. I'd come instead of going to school. If they weren't hitting, he'd start talking to them, singing them songs."

"Like what?" Eddie said.

"He'd make them up. They were funny, man. It don't come across in English: 'Little silver ones fill up my shoes. My heart is lonesome for the fish of the sea.' It was like very formal how he'd say it. He'd always call this the sea. I'd tell him it's a lake, but he couldn't be talked out of it. He was very stubborn—too stubborn to learn English. I ain't been fishing since he went back to Mexico."

They walked to the end of the pier, then back past the fishermen. A lot of them were old men gently tug-ging lines between their fingers, lifting nets as if flying underwater kites, plucking the wriggling silver fish from the netting, the yellow light of their lamps glinting off the bright scales.

"I told you they were out here," Manny said.

They sat on a concrete ledge, staring at the dark water, which rocked hypnotically below the soles of their dangling feet.

"Feel like diving in?" Manny asked.

Eddie had just raised the bottle to his lips and paused as if actually considering Manny's question, then shook his head no and took a swallow.

"One time right before my uncle went back to Mexico we came fishing at night for perch," Manny said. "It was a real hot night, you know? And all these old guys fishing off the pier. No one getting a bite, man, and I started thinking how cool and peaceful it would be to just dive in the water with the fish, and then, like I just did it without even deciding to, clothes and all. Sometimes, man, I still remember that feeling underwater—like I could just keep swimming out, didn't need air, never had to come up. When I couldn't hold my breath no more and came up I could hear my uncle calling my name, and then all the old guys on the pier start calling my name to come back. What I really felt like doing was to keep swimming out until I couldn't hear them, until I couldn't even see their lanterns, man. I wanted to be way the fuck out alone in the middle of the lake when the sun came up. But then I thought about my uncle standing on the pier calling me, so I turned around."

They killed the bottle sitting on a concrete ledge and dropped it into the lake. Then they rode the El back. It was getting lighter without a dawn. The El windows were streaked with rain, the Douglas Avenue station smelled wet. It was a dark morning. They should have ended it then. Instead they sat at Manny's kitchen table drinking instant coffee with canned milk. Eddie kept getting lost in the designs the milk would make, swirls and thunderclouds in his mug of coffee. He was numb and shaky. His jaw ached.

"I'm really crashin'," he told Manny.

"Here," Manny said. "Bring us down easier, man."

"I don't like doing downers, man," Eddie said.

"'Ludes," Manny said, "from Pancho's stash."

They sat across the table from each other for a long time—talking, telling their memories and secrets—only Eddie was too numb to remember exactly what they said. Their voices—his own as well as Manny's—seemed *outside*, removed from the center of his mind.

At one point Manny looked out at the dark morning and said, "It still seems like last night."

"That's right," Eddie agreed. He wanted to say more but couldn't express it. He didn't try. Eddie didn't believe it was what they said that was important. Manny could be talking Spanish; I could be talking Polish, Eddie thought. It didn't matter. What meant something was sitting at the table together, wrecked together, still awake watching the rainy light spatter the window, walking out again, to the Prague bakery for bismarcks, past people under dripping umbrellas on their way to church.

"Looks like Sunday," Manny said.

"Today's Friday," Eddie said. "It's Good Friday."

"I seen ladies with ashes on their heads waiting for the bus a couple days ago," Manny told him.

They stood in the doorway of the Prague, out of the rain, eating their bismarcks. Just down from the church, the bakery was a place people crowded into after mass. Its windows displayed colored eggs and little frosted Easter lambs.

"One time on Ash Wednesday I was eating a bismarck and Pancho made a cross on my forehead with the powdered sugar like it was ashes. When I went to church the priest wouldn't give me real ashes," Manny said with a grin.

It was one of the few times Eddie had heard Manny mention Pancho. Now that they were outside, Eddie's head felt clearer than it had in the kitchen.

"I used to try and keep my ashes on until Good Friday," he told Manny, "but they'd make me wash."

The church bells were ringing, echoes bouncing off the sidewalks as if deflected by the ceiling of clouds. The neighborhood felt narrower, compressed from above.

"I wonder if it still looks the same in there," Manny said as they passed the church.

They stepped in and stood in the vestibule. The saints of their childhood stood shrouded in purple. The altar was bare, stripped for Good Friday. Old ladies, ignoring the new liturgy, chanted a litany in Polish.

"Same as ever," Eddie whispered as they backed out.

The rain had almost let up. They could hear its accumulated weight in the wing-flaps of pigeons.

"Good Friday was Pancho's favorite holiday, man," Manny said. "Everybody else always picked Christmas or Thanksgiving or Fourth of July. He hadda be different, man. I remember he used to drag me along visiting churches. You ever do that?"

"Hell, yeah," Eddie said. "Every Good Friday we'd go on our bikes. You hadda visit seven of them."

Without agreeing to it they walked from St. Roman's to St. Michael's, a little wooden Franciscan church in an Italian neighborhood; and from there to St. Casimir's, a towering, mournful church with twin copper-green towers. Then, as if following an invisible trail, they walked north up Twenty-second toward St. Anne's, St.

Puis's, St. Adalbert's. At first they merely entered and left immediately, as if touching base, but their familiarity with small rituals quickly returned: dipping their fingers in the holy water font by the door, making the automatic sign of the cross as they passed the life-size crucified Christs that hung in the vestibules where old women and school kids clustered to kiss the spikes in the bronze or bloody plaster feet. By St. Anne's, Manny removed his sunglasses, out of respect, the way one removes a hat. Eddie put them on. His eyes felt hard-boiled. The surge of energy he had felt at the bakery had burned out fast. While Manny genuflected to the altar, Eddie slumped in the back pew pretending to pray, drowsing off behind the dark glasses. It never occurred to Eddie to simply go home. His head ached, he could feel his heart racing, and would suddenly jolt awake wondering where Manny was. Manny would be off— jumpy, frazzled, still popping speed on the sly—exploring the church as if searching for something, standing among lines of parishioners waiting to kiss relics the priest wiped repeatedly clean with a rag of silk. Then Manny would be shaking Eddie awake. "How you holding up, man?"

"I'm cool," he'd say, and they would be back on the streets heading for another parish under the overcast sky. Clouds, a shade between slate and lilac, smoked over the spires and roofs; lights flashed on in the bars and *taquerías*. On Eighteenth Street a great blue neon fish leapt in the storefront window of a tiny *ostenaria*. Eddie tried to note the exact location to add to his window collection. They headed along a wall of viaducts to St. Procopius, where, Manny said, both he and Pancho had been baptized. The viaduct walls had been painted by schoolchildren into a mural that seemed to go for miles.

"I don't think we're gonna make seven churches, man," Eddie said. He was walking without lifting his feet, his hair plastered by a sweatlike drizzle. It was around 3:00 p.m. It had been 3:00 p.m.—Christ's dark hour on the cross—inside the churches all day, but now it was turning 3:00 p.m. outside too. They could hear the ancient-sounding hymn "Tantum Ergo," carrying from down the block.

Eddie sunk into the last pew, kneeling in the red glow of vigil lights that brought back the red flicker of the flares they had seen from the window of the bus as it sped by the prison. Manny had already faded into the procession making the stations of the cross—a shuffling crowd circling the church, kneeling before each station while altar boys censed incense and the priest recited Christ's agony. Old women answered with prayers like moans.

Old women were walking on their knees up the marble aisle to kiss the relics. A few were crying, and Eddie remembered how back in grade school he had heard old women cry sometimes after confession, crying as if their hearts would break, and even as a child he had wondered how such old women could possibly have committed sins terrible enough to demand such bitter weeping. Most everything from that world had changed or disappeared, but the old women had endured—Polish, Bohemian, Spanish, he knew it didn't matter; they were the same, dressed in black coats and babushkas the way holy statues wore violet, in constant mourning. A common pain of loss seemed to burn at the core of their lives, though Eddie had never understood exactly what

it was they mourned. Nor how day after day they had
sustained the intensity of their grief. He would have
given up long ago. In a way he *had* given up, and the
ache left behind couldn't be called grief. He had no name
for it. He had felt it before Pancho or anyone was lost,
almost from the start of memory. If it was grief; it was
grief for the living. The hymns, with their ancient, keening
melodies and mysterious words, had brought the feeling
back, but when he tried to discover the source, to give
the feeling a name, it eluded him as always, leaving in its
place nostalgia and triggered nerves.

Oh God, he prayed, I'm really crashing.

He was too shaky to kneel, so he stretched out on
the pew, lying on his back, eyes shut behind sunglasses,
until the church began to whirl. To control it he tried
concentrating on the stained-glass window overhead.
None of the windows that had ever been special for him
were from a church. This one was an angel, its colors
like jewels and coals. Afternoon seemed to be dying
behind it, becoming part of the night, part of the private
history that he and Manny continued between them like
a pact. He could see night shining through the colors of
the angel, dividing into bands as if the angel were a
prism for darkness; the neon and wet streetlights illuminated its wingspread.


## LEGENDS

It started with ice.

That's how Big Antek sometimes began the story.

At dusk a gang of little Mexican kids appeared with

a few lumps of dry ice covered in a shoe box, as if they had caught a bird. *Hot ice*, they called it, though the way they said it sounded to Antek like *hot eyes*. Kids always have a way of finding stuff like that. One boy touched his tongue to a piece and screamed *"Aye!"* when it stuck. They watched the ice boil and fume in a rain puddle along the curb, and finally they filled a bottle part way with water, inserted the fragments of ice they had left, capped the bottle, and set it in the mouth of an alley waiting for an explosion. When it popped they scattered.

Manny Santora and Eddie Kapusta came walking up the alley, wanting Antek to buy them a bottle of rum at Buddy's. Rum instead of beer. They were celebrating, Kapusta said, but he didn't say what. Maybe one of them had found a job or had just been fired, or graduated, or joined the army instead of waiting around to get drafted. It could be anything. They were always celebrating. Behind their sunglasses Antek could see they were high as usual, even before Manny offered him a drag off a reefer the size of a cigar.

Probably nobody was hired or fired or had joined anything; probably it was just so hot they had a good excuse to act crazy. They each had a bottle of Coke they were fizzing up, squirting. Eddie had limes stuffed in his pockets and was pretending they were his balls. Manny had a plastic bag of the little ice cubes they sell at gas stations. It was half-melted, and they were scooping handfuls of cubes over each other's heads, stuffing them down their jeans and yowling, rubbing ice on their chests and under their arms as if taking a cold shower. They looked like wild men—shirts hanging from their back pockets, handkerchiefs knotted around their heads, wearing sunglasses, their bodies slick with melted ice water and sweat; two guys in the prime of life going nowhere, both lean, Kapusta almost as tan as Santora, Santora with that frizzy beard under his lip, and Kapusta trying to juggle limes.

They were drinking rum using a method Antek had never seen before, and he had seen his share of drinking—not just in the neighborhood—all over the world when he was in the navy, and not the Bohemian navy either like somebody would always say when he would start telling navy stories.

They claimed they were drinking cuba libres, only they didn't have glasses, so they were mixing the drinks in their mouths, starting with some little cubes, then pouring in rum, Coke, a squeeze of lime, and swallowing. Swallowing if one or the other didn't suddenly bust up over some private joke, spraying the whole mouthful out, and both of them choking and coughing and laughing.

"Hey, Antek, lemme build you a drink," Manny kept saying, but Antek shook his head no thanks, and he wasn't known for passing up too many.

This was all going on in front of Buddy's, everyone catching a blast of music and air-conditioning whenever the door opened. It was hot. The moths sizzled as soon as they hit Buddy's buzzing orange sign. A steady beat of moths dropped like cinders on the blinking orange sidewalk where the kids were pitching pennies. Manny passed around what was left in the plastic bag of ice, and the kids stood sucking and crunching the cubes between their teeth.

It reminded Antek of summers when the ice trucks

still delivered to Buddy's—flatbeds covered with canvas, the icemen, mainly DPs, wearing leather aprons. Their Popeye forearms, even in August, looked ruddy with cold. They would slide the huge, clear blocks off the tailgate so the whump reverberated through the hollow under the sidewalks, and deep in the ice the clarity shattered. Then with their ice hooks they'd lug the blocks across the sidewalk, trailing a slick, and boot them skidding down the chute into Buddy's beery-smelling cellar. And after the truck pulled away, kids would pick the splinters from the curb and suck them as if they were ice-flavored Popsicles.

Nobody seemed too interested when Antek tried to tell them about the ice trucks, or anything else about how the world had been, for that matter. Antek had been sick and had only recently returned from the VA hospital. Of all his wounds, sickness was the worst. He could examine his hacked butcher's hands almost as kids from the neighborhood did, inspecting the stubs where his fingers had been as if they belonged to someone else, but there were places deep within himself that he couldn't examine, yet where he could feel that something of himself far more essential than fingers was missing. He returned from the VA feeling old and as if the neighborhood had changed in the weeks he had been gone. People had changed. He couldn't be sure, but they treated him differently, colder, as if he were becoming a stranger in the place he had grown up in, now, just when he most needed to belong.

"Hey, Antek," Manny said, "you know what you can tell me? That girl that saved your life in the meat freezer, did she have good tits?"

"I tell you about a miracle and you ask me about tits?" Antek said. "I don't talk about that anymore because now somebody always asks me did she have good tits. Go see."

Kids had been trying for years to sneak into the icehouse to see her. It was what the neighborhood had instead of a haunted house. Each generation had grown up with the story of how her father had ridden with her half-naked body on the streetcar. Even the nuns had heard Antek's story about finding the girl still frozen in the meat freezer. The butcher shop in Kedzie had closed long ago, and the legend was that after the cops had stopped checking, her body had been moved at night back into the icehouse. But the icehouse wasn't easy to break into. It had stood padlocked and heavily boarded for years.

"They're gonna wreck it," Eddie said. "I went by on the bus and they got the crane out in front."

"Uh-oh, last chance, Antek," Manny said. "If you're sure she's in there, maybe we oughta go save her."

"She's in there," Antek said. He noticed the little kids had stopped pitching pennies and were listening.

"Well, you owe her something after what she done for you—don't he, Eduardo?"

The kids who were listening chuckled, then started to go back to their pennies.

"You wanna go, I'll go!" Antek said loudly.

"All right, let's go."

Antek got up unsteadily. He stared at Eddie and Manny. "You guys couldn't loan me enough for a taste of wine just until I get my disability check?"

The little kids tagged after them to the end of the

block, then turned back bored. Manny and Eddie kept going, picking the pace up a step or two ahead of Antek, exchanging looks and grinning. But Antek knew that no matter how much they joked or what excuses they gave, they were going, like him, for one last look. They were just old enough to have seen the icehouse before it shut down. It was a special building, the kind a child couldn't help but notice and remember—there, on the corner across the street from the prison, a factory that made ice, humming with fans, its louvered roof dripping and clacking, lost in acrid clouds of its own escaping vapor.

The automatic ice machine in front had already been carted away. The doors were still padlocked, but the way the crane was parked it was possible for Manny and Eddie to climb the boom onto the roof.

Antek waited below. He gazed up at the new Plexiglas guard turrets on the prison wall. From his angle all he could see was the bluish fluorescence of their lighting. He watched Manny and Eddie jump from the boom to the roof, high enough to stare across at the turrets like snipers, to draw a level bead on the backs of the guards, high enough to gaze over the wall at the dim, barred windows of the buildings that resembled foundries more than ever in the sweltering heat.

Below, Antek stood swallowing wine, expecting more from the night than a condemned building. He didn't know exactly what else he expected. Perhaps only a scent, like the stab of remembered ammonia he might have detected if he were still young enough to climb the boom. Perhaps the secret isolation he imagined Manny and Eddie feeling now, alone on the roof, as if lost in clouds of vapor. At street level, passing traffic drowned out the tick of a single cricket keeping time on the roof—a cricket so loud and insistent that Manny didn't stop to worry about the noise when he kicked in the louvers. And Antek, though he had once awakened in a freezer, couldn't imagine the shock of cold that Manny and Eddie felt as they dropped out of the summer night to the floor below.

Earlier, on their way down Twenty-sixth, Manny had stopped to pick up an unused flare from along the tracks, and Antek pictured them inside now, Manny, his hand wrapped in a handkerchief, holding the flare away from him like a Roman candle, its red glare sputtering off the beams and walls.

There wasn't much to see—empty corners, insulated pipes. Their breaths steamed. They tugged on their shirts. Instinctively, they traced the cold down a metal staircase. Cold was rising from the ground floor through the soles of their gym shoes.

The ground floor was stacked to the ceiling with junked ice machines. A wind as from an enormous air conditioner was blowing down a narrow aisle between the machines. At the end of the aisle a concrete ramp slanted down to the basement.

That was where Antek suspected they would end up, the basement, a cavernous space extending under the nameless street, slowly collapsing as if the thick, melting pillars of ice along its walls had served as its foundation. The floor was spongy with waterlogged sawdust. An echoing rain plipped from the ceiling. The air smelled thawed, and ached clammy in the lungs.

"It's fuckin' freezing," Eddie whispered.

Manny swung the flare in a slow arc, its reflections glancing as if they stood among cracked mirrors. Blocks

of ice, framed in defrosted freezer coils, glowed back
faintly, like aquarium windows, from niches along the
walls. They were melting unevenly and leaned at precari-
ous angles. Several had already tottered to the sawdust,
where they lay like quarry stones from a wrecked
cathedral. Manny and Eddie picked their way among
them, pausing to wipe the slick of water from their
surfaces and peer into the ice, but deep networks of
cracks refracted the light. They could see only frozen
shadows and had to guess at the forms: fish, birds,
shanks of meat, a dog, a cat, a chair, what appeared to
be a bicycle.

But Antek knew they would recognize her when they
found her. There would be no mistaking the light. In the
smoky, phosphorous glare her hair would reflect gold like
a candle behind a frosted pane. He was waiting for them to
bring her out. He had finished the wine and flung the pint
bottle onto the street so that it shattered. The streets were
empty. He was waiting patiently, and though he had
nowhere else to be it was still a long wait. He would wait
as long as it might take, but even so he wondered if there
was time enough left to him for another miracle in his life.
He could hear the cricket now, composing time instead
of music, working its way headfirst from the roof down
the brick wall. Listening to it, Antek became acutely aware
of the silence of the prison across the street. He thought
of all the men on the other side of the wall and wondered
how many were still awake, listening to the cricket,
waiting patiently as they sweated in the heavy night.

Manny and Eddie, shivering, their hands burning
numb from grappling with ice, unbarred the rear door
that opened onto the loading platform behind the ice-

house. They pushed out an old handcar and rolled it onto the tracks that came right up to the dock. They had already slid the block of ice onto the handcar and draped it with a canvas tarp. Even gently inching it on they had heard the ice cracking. The block of ice had felt too light for its size, fragile, ready to break apart.

"It feels like we're kidnapping somebody," Eddie whispered.

"Just think of it as ice."

"I can't."

"We can't just leave her here, Eduardo."

"What'll we do with her?"

"We'll think of something."

"What about Antek?"

"Forget him."

They pushed off. Rust slowed them at first, but as the tracks inclined toward the river they gained momentum. It was like learning to row. By the trestle they hit their rhythm. Speed became wind—hair blowing, shirts flapping open, the tarp billowing up off the ice. The skyline gleamed ahead, and though Manny couldn't see the lake, he could feel it stretching beyond the skyscrapers; he could recall the sudden lightness of freedom he'd felt once when he had speared out underwater and glided effortlessly away, one moment expanding into another, while the flow of water cleansed him of memory, and not even the sound of his own breath disrupted the silence. The smelt would have disappeared to wherever they disappeared to, but the fishermen would still be sitting at the edge of the breakwater, their backs to the city, dreaming up fish. And if the fishermen still remembered his name, they might call it again repeatedly in a chorus of voices echoing out over the dark surface of the water, but this time, Manny knew, there would be no turning back. He knew now where they were taking her, where she would finally be released. They were rushing through waist-deep weeds, crossing the vast tracts of prairie behind the factories, clattering over bridges and viaducts. Below, streetlights shimmered watery in the old industrial neighborhoods. Shiny with sweat, the girl already melting free between them, they forced themselves faster, rowing like a couple of sailors.

# LOST

I remember, though I might have dreamed it, a radio show I listened to when we lived on Eighteenth Street above the taxidermist. It was a program in which kids phoned the station and reported something they'd lost — a code ring, a cap gun, a ball, a doll — always their favorite. And worse than lost toys, pets, not just dogs and cats, but hamsters, parakeets, dime store turtles with painted shells.

I'd tune to the program by accident, then forget about it, and each time I rediscovered it, it made me feel as if I were reliving the time before. The lost pets would always make me think of the old Hungarian downstairs who, people said, skinned stray cats, and of my secret pets, the foxes in his murky shop window, their glass eyes glittering fiercely from a dusty jungle of ferns, and their lips retracted in a constant snarl.

Magically, by the end of the program, everything would be found. I still don't know how they accomplished this, and recall wondering if it would work to phone in and report something I'd always wanted as missing. For it seemed to me then that something one always wanted, but never had, was his all the same, and wasn't it lost?

# PET MILK

Today I've been drinking instant coffee and Pet milk, and watching it snow. It's not that I enjoy the taste especially, but I like the way Pet milk swirls in the coffee. Actually, my favorite thing about Pet milk is what the can opener does to the top of the can. The can is unmistakable—compact, seamless looking, its very shape suggesting that it could condense milk without any trouble. The can opener bites in neatly, and the thick liquid spills from the triangular gouge with a different look and viscosity than milk. Pet milk isn't *real* milk. The color's off, to start with. There's almost something of the past about it, like old ivory. My grandmother always drank it in her coffee. When friends dropped over and sat around the kitchen table, my grandma would ask, "Do you take cream and sugar?" Pet milk was the cream.

There was a yellow plastic radio on her kitchen table, usually tuned to the polka station, though sometimes she'd miss it by half a notch and get the Greek station instead, or the Spanish, or the Ukrainian. In Chicago, where we lived, all the incompatible states of Europe were pressed together down at the staticky right end of the dial. She didn't seem to notice, as long as she wasn't hearing English. The radio, turned low, played constantly. Its top was warped and turning amber on the side where the tubes were. I remember the sound of it on winter afternoons after school, as I sat by her table watching the Pet milk swirl and cloud in the steaming coffee, and noticing, outside her window, the sky doing the same thing above the railroad yard across the street.

And I remember, much later, seeing the same swirling sky in tiny liqueur glasses containing a drink called a King Alphonse: the crème de cacao rising like smoke in repeated explosions, blooming in kaleidoscopic clouds through the layer of heavy cream. This was in the Pilsen, a little Czech restaurant where my girlfriend, Kate, and I would go sometimes in the evening. It was the first year out of college for both of us, and we had astonished ourselves by finding real jobs—no more waitressing or pumping gas, the way we'd done in school. I was investigating credit references at a bank, and she was doing something slightly above the rank of typist for Hornblower & Weeks, the investment firm. My bank showed training films that emphasized the importance of suitable dress, good grooming, and personal neatness, even for employees like me, who worked at the switchboard in the basement. Her firm issued directives on appropriate attire—skirts, for instance, should cover the knees. She had lovely knees.

Kate and I would sometimes meet after work at the

Pilsen, dressed in our proper business clothes and still feeling both a little self-conscious and glamorous, as if we were impostors wearing disguises. The place had small, round oak tables, and we'd sit in a corner under a painting called "The Street Musicians of Prague" and trade future plans as if they were escape routes. She talked of going to grad school in Europe; I wanted to apply to the Peace Corps. Our plans for the future made us laugh and feel close, but those same plans somehow made anything more than temporary between us seem impossible. It was the first time I'd ever had the feeling of missing someone I was still with.

The waiters in the Pilsen wore short black jackets over long white aprons. They were old men from the old country. We went there often enough to have our own special waiter, Rudi, a name he pronounced with a rolled *R*. Rudi boned our trout and seasoned our salads, and at the end of the meal he'd bring the bottle of crème de cacao from the bar, along with two little glasses and a small pitcher of heavy cream, and make us each a King Alphonse right at our table. We'd watch as he'd fill the glasses halfway up with the syrupy brown liqueur, then carefully attempt to float a layer of cream on top. If he failed to float the cream, we'd get that one free.

"Who was King Alphonse anyway, Rudi?" I sometimes asked, trying to break his concentration, and if that didn't work I nudged the table with my foot so the glass would jiggle imperceptibly just as he was floating the cream. We'd usually get one on the house. Rudi knew what I was doing. In fact, serving the King Alphonses had been his idea, and he had also suggested the trick of jarring the table. I think it pleased him, though he seemed concerned about the way I'd stare into the liqueur glass, watching the patterns.

"It's not a microscope," he'd say. "Drink."

He liked us, and we tipped extra. It felt good to be there and to be able to pay for a meal.

Kate and I met at the Pilsen for supper on my twenty-second birthday. It was May, and unseasonably hot. I'd opened my tie. Even before looking at the dinner menu, we ordered a bottle of Mumm's and a dozen oysters apiece. Rudi made a sly remark when he brought the oysters on platters of ice. They were freshly opened and smelled of the sea. I'd heard people joke about oysters being aphrodisiac but never considered it anything but a myth—the kind of idea they still had in the old country.

We squeezed on lemon, added dabs of horseradish, slid the oysters into our mouths, and then rinsed the shells with champagne and drank the salty, cold juice. There was a beefy-looking couple eating schnitzel at the next table, and they stared at us with the repugnance that public oyster-eaters in the Midwest often encounter. We laughed and grandly sipped it all down. I was already half tipsy from drinking too fast, and starting to feel filled with a euphoric, aching energy. Kate raised a brimming oyster shell to me in a toast: "To the Peace Corps!"

"To Europe!" I replied, and we clunked shells.

She touched her wineglass to mine and whispered, "Happy birthday," and then suddenly leaned across the table and kissed me.

When she sat down again, she was flushed. I caught the reflection of her face in the glass-covered "The Street Musicians of Prague" above our table. I always loved seeing her in mirrors and windows. The reflections of her beauty startled me. I had told her that once, and she seemed to fend off the compliment, saying, "That's because you've learned what to look for," as if it were a secret I'd stumbled upon. But, this time, seeing her reflection hovering ghostlike upon an imaginary Prague was like seeing a future from which she had vanished. I knew I'd never meet anyone more beautiful to me.

We killed the champagne and sat twining fingers across the table. I was sweating. I could feel the warmth of her through her skirt under the table and I touched her leg. We still hadn't ordered dinner. I left money on the table and we steered each other out a little unsteadily.

"Rudi will understand," I said.

The street was blindingly bright. A reddish sun angled just above the rims of the tallest buildings. I took my suit coat off and flipped it over my shoulder. We stopped in the doorway of a shoe store to kiss.

"Let's go somewhere," she said.

My roommate would already be home at my place, which was closer. Kate lived up north, in Evanston. It seemed a long way away.

We cut down a side street, past a fire station, to a small park, but its gate was locked. I pressed close to her against the tall iron fence. We could smell the lilacs from a bush just inside the fence, and when I jumped for an overhanging branch my shirt sleeve hooked on a fence spike and tore, and petals rained down on us as the sprig sprang from my hand.

We walked to the subway. The evening rush was winding down; we must have caught the last express heading toward Evanston. Once the train climbed from the tunnel to the elevated tracks, it wouldn't stop until the end of the line, on Howard. There weren't any seats together, so we stood swaying at the front of the car, beside the empty conductor's compartment. We wedged inside, and I clicked the door shut.

The train rocked and jounced, clattering north. We were kissing, trying to catch the rhythm of the ride with our bodies. The sun bronzed the windows on our side of the train. I lifted her skirt over her knees, hiked it higher so the sun shone off her thighs, and bunched it around her waist. She wouldn't stop kissing. She was moving her hips to pin us to each jolt of the train.

We were speeding past scorched brick walls, gray windows, back porches outlined in sun, roofs, and treetops—the landscape of the El I'd memorized from subway windows over a lifetime of rides: the podiatrist's foot sign past Fullerton; the bright pennants of Wrigley Field, at Addison; ancient hotels with TRANSIENTS WEL-COME signs on their flaking back walls; peeling and graffiti-smudged billboards; the old cemetery just before Wilson Avenue. Even without looking, I knew almost exactly where we were. Within the compartment, the sound of our quick breathing was louder than the clatter of tracks. I was trying to slow down, to make it all last, and when she covered my mouth with her hand I turned my face to the window and looked out.

The train was braking a little from express speed, as it did each time it passed a local station. I could see blurred faces on the long wooden platform watching us pass—businessmen glancing up from folded newspapers, women clutching purses and shopping bags. I could see the expression on each face, momentarily arrested, as we flashed by. A high school kid in shirt sleeves, maybe sixteen, with books tucked under one arm and a cigarette in his mouth, caught sight of us, and in the instant before he disappeared he grinned and started to wave. Then he was gone, and I turned from the window, back to Kate, forgetting everything—the passing stations, the glowing late sky, even the sense of missing her—but that arrested wave stayed with me. It was as if I were standing on that platform, with my schoolbooks and a smoke, on one of those endlessly accumulated afternoons after school when I stood almost outside of time simply waiting for a train, and I thought how much I'd have loved seeing someone like us streaming by.

## ABOUT THE AUTHOR

Stuart Dybek was born and raised in Chicago. His stories and poems have appeared in many magazines, including *The Atlantic Monthly, The Iowa Review, The New Yorker, Antaeus,* and *Ploughshares.* Mr. Dybek was awarded the Whiting Writers Award in 1984. Three of the stories in *The Coast of Chicago* appeared in the O. Henry prize story collections: "Hot Ice" (which won first prize) in 1985, "Pet Milk" in 1986, and "Blight" in 1987. He is also the author of another work of fiction, *Childhood and Other Neighborhoods* (1980), and a book of poems, *Brass Knuckles* (1979). Mr. Dybek lives in Kalamazoo, Michigan, with his wife and two children and teaches English at Western Michigan University.

# VINTAGE
# CONTEMPORARIES

| | | |
|---|---|---|
| ___ **I Pass Like Night** by Jonathan Ames | $8.95 | 679-72857-0 |
| ___ **The Mezzanine** by Nicholson Baker | $7.95 | 679-72576-8 |
| ___ **Room Temperature** by Nicholson Baker | $9.00 | 679-73440-6 |
| ___ **Chilly Scenes of Winter** by Ann Beattie | $9.95 | 679-73234-9 |
| ___ **Distortions** by Ann Beattie | $9.95 | 679-73235-7 |
| ___ **Falling in Place** by Ann Beattie | $10.00 | 679-73192-X |
| ___ **Love Always** by Ann Beattie | $7.95 | 394-74418-7 |
| ___ **Picturing Will** by Ann Beattie | $9.95 | 679-73194-6 |
| ___ **Secrets and Surprises** by Ann Beattie | $10.00 | 679-73193-8 |
| ___ **A Farm Under a Lake** by Martha Bergland | $9.95 | 679-73011-7 |
| ___ **The History of Luminous Motion** by Scott Bradfield | $8.95 | 679-72943-7 |
| ___ **First Love and Other Sorrows** by Harold Brodkey | $7.95 | 679-72075-8 |
| ___ **Stories in an Almost Classical Mode** by Harold Brodkey | $12.95 | 679-72431-1 |
| ___ **The Debut** by Anita Brookner | $8.95 | 679-72712-4 |
| ___ **Latecomers** by Anita Brookner | $8.95 | 679-72668-3 |
| ___ **Lewis Percy** by Anita Brookner | $10.00 | 679-72944-5 |
| ___ **Dirty Work** by Larry Brown | $9.95 | 679-73049-4 |
| ___ **Harry and Catherine** by Frederick Busch | $10.00 | 679-73076-1 |
| ___ **Sleeping in Flame** by Jonathan Carroll | $8.95 | 679-72777-9 |
| ___ **Cathedral** by Raymond Carver | $8.95 | 679-72369-2 |
| ___ **Fires** by Raymond Carver | $8.95 | 679-72239-4 |
| ___ **What We Talk About When We Talk About Love** by Raymond Carver | $8.95 | 679-72305-6 |
| ___ **Where I'm Calling From** by Raymond Carver | $9.95 | 679-72231-9 |
| ___ **The House on Mango Street** by Sandra Cisneros | $9.00 | 679-73477-5 |
| ___ **I Look Divine** by Christopher Coe | $5.95 | 394-75995-8 |
| ___ **Dancing Bear** by James Crumley | $6.95 | 394-72576-X |
| ___ **The Last Good Kiss** by James Crumley | $9.95 | 394-75989-3 |
| ___ **One to Count Cadence** by James Crumley | $9.95 | 394-73559-5 |
| ___ **The Wrong Case** by James Crumley | $7.95 | 394-73558-7 |
| ___ **The Colorist** by Susan Daitch | $8.95 | 679-72492-3 |
| ___ **The Last Election** by Pete Davies | $6.95 | 394-74702-X |
| ___ **Great Jones Street** by Don DeLillo | $7.95 | 679-72303-X |
| ___ **The Names** by Don DeLillo | $10.95 | 679-72295-5 |
| ___ **Players** by Don DeLillo | $7.95 | 679-72293-9 |
| ___ **Ratner's Star** by Don DeLillo | $8.95 | 679-72292-0 |
| ___ **Running Dog** by Don DeLillo | $7.95 | 679-72294-7 |
| ___ **The Commitments** by Roddy Doyle | $6.95 | 679-72174-6 |
| ___ **Selected Stories** by Andre Dubus | $10.95 | 679-72533-4 |
| ___ **The Coast of Chicago** by Stuart Dybek | $9.00 | 679-73334-5 |
| ___ **From Rockaway** by Jill Eisenstadt | $6.95 | 394-75761-0 |

# VINTAGE
# CONTEMPORARIES

# VINTAGE
# CONTEMPORARIES